# UNDER THE RADAR
# PETER CUMYN

Pitullie Publishers

Pitullie Publishers

Under the Radar



ISBN 978-1-7780009-4-2 (paperback)
ISBN 978-1-7780009-5-9 (ebook)

Cover design and illustrations by Paul Abraham
Interior formatting by Aaxel Author Group

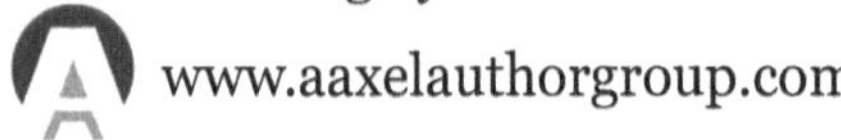

www.aaxelauthorgroup.com

*This is a work of fiction. Names, characters, events and incidents are the products of the author's imagination. Any resemblance to actual persons, living or dead, or actual events is purely coincidental.*

To my wife Madeleine,
our children and grandchildren.

1

Sergeant Detective Carmel Roch of the Montreal Police led the way into the dark stairwell of the building. She didn't remove her pistol from its holster, but gave it a quick pat, just to reassure herself that it was there. Turning behind, she motioned to the other two officers to approach, and when it was clear that the three of them were ready to move, she gave them a silent thumbs-up.

Carmel loved these moments. They were an opportunity to live life to the hilt. All of the elements were there: risk; the unknown; a situation to figure out; decisions to be taken rapidly. She was like a surgeon repairing a ruptured artery, a pilot landing in a terrible crosswind, a lawyer in court confronted by an awkward question from the bench. Above all, she was in charge.

"Let's go, boys," she whispered in a low voice as they started up the stairs. "Be ready. There could be trouble. You never know."

Carmel was tall and broad-shouldered, big, but certainly not overweight. She had medium-length brown hair that she often tied up in a ponytail, and a face that was open and frank, with intelligent eyes and a long straight nose. When she smiled, it was not for show—it really meant something. The police uniform suited her too. It made her look smart, and sharp, like somebody to be trusted, but not to be trifled with.

There was a streak of idealism in Carmel. She felt strongly that it was her responsibility to protect the public from harm, and to show her junior colleagues how to act. It came to her naturally, the wish to serve, and the instinct to act as a role model.

Her two colleagues were close behind and had to move smartly in order to keep up. Charles Gagné was pretty solid, pretty reliable. He had worked on a number of cases with Carmel, usually acting as her backup man, her gopher, someone who followed up on leads and filed reports. The other officer, Jean Perras, looked nervous. He was fairly new to the force. She knew him less, but he seemed alright.

She checked her cellphone. Eighteen minutes after five. Not a bad response. The call had come into the station at four thirty-nine. "There's been a murder," the caller had said, in a man's voice. "Fourth floor, in the hallway outside the door of the penthouse." He had then given the address, a street down near the Lachine Canal. The officer who took the call said that the caller had sounded pretty agitated.

There was a smell of dampness and fresh paint in the stairwell, and it was difficult to avoid making a clanging noise on the metal stairs. Carmel noticed with approval that the walls were spotlessly clean. The building was brand new, after all. In fact, it was still under construction. The lighting didn't seem to be working very well, so she flicked the light of her cellphone on from time to time in order to be sure of the way forward.

When the three officers reached the top of the first

flight of stairs, they paused to listen. Within the stairwell, there was only a muted, hollowed-out version of the city's background murmur, an amalgam of cars moving down the Bonaventure Expressway, of containers being shifted under huge cranes in the Port of Montreal, of small children shouting together in the courtyards of their day-care centres and of jackhammers gnawing at the bedrock to create footings for yet new skyscrapers to appear.

The only actual, identifiable sound that the three officers could hear was that of their own breathing.

They started on up again. There were eighteen steps to each flight of stairs. Carmel counted them subconsciously, "eight, nine, ten, eleven…" her hand gliding up the railing, barely touching it, just feeling that it was there, letting it guide her and give her reassurance. The three of them formed a phalanx, walking in step, peering up above to see what lay around the next twist of stairs.

With the Canadian army in Afghanistan, Carmel had experienced moments like this, particularly when she had led patrols through the small villages outside Kandahar—moments of tension and suspense, when you didn't know what to expect, or what would happen next. Sometimes, a chicken would simply appear and run off through the dust, flapping its wings and squawking noisily. Sometimes they would come across a woman and her children, huddled speechless and terrified in a dark recess of their shattered home. Sometimes, though, there would be trouble, and the patrol would have to hole up somewhere and call for support.

She realised that her left hand was tightly clenched and damp with sweat, a reaction to the tension of the moment. "Relax, Carmy," she told herself. "Just relax." On the other hand, she knew that it didn't pay to be casual—you had to remain on your guard. She opened and shut the hand several times.

On the last landing, a weak light filtered through from a skylight above, and there were several sheets of plasterboard propped up against the wall and a white pail of scrap on the floor. The three officers paused in front of a grey metal door. Carmel turned one last time to check on her companions. Charles Gagné gave her a quick smile and shrugged his shoulders, gesturing towards the door and the hallway beyond. He adored Carmel. His faith in her knew no limits. Where she would go, so would he.

Perras gave her a reassuring nod. He was okay. "Go on, open the door," he seemed to say.

She gradually opened the heavy metal door and peered into the ill-lit hallway. There was a smell of freshly laid carpeting, but nothing to be seen, nothing to be heard. "Police," she shouted, and the three stepped quickly forward, Gagné and Perras taking up positions on each side of her. "This way," she said to them, pointing to their left.

They rounded a corner of the hallway and stopped almost at once. At their feet lay a body, the body of a man. A pool of congealed blood had formed next to him, and small amounts of blood still appeared to be oozing out from under a shoulder. His legs were splayed crookedly apart, and one arm was thrown to the side. Carmel glanced at his face. It was pale grey, and the mouth was distorted, as though the victim had wanted to say something, or at least to scream in protest or in anger at the moment before his life was extinguished. His head was covered with curls of nearly blonde hair which were now glued together in a sticky sweat. He was wearing a pink shirt, which was partially pulled up towards his neck and stained with blood, and his pale blue slacks were wet between the legs. You could smell both the blood and the urine.

She turned to the others. Perras looked like he was

POLICE
CARMEL KALLAN
POLICE

about to puke. "You guys check in there," she said to them, pointing to the open door leading from the hallway into the apartment. "Be careful, stay together, and don't touch things more than you have to." She kneeled beside the body and checked for any signs of life, but there were none.

The victim was white, in his late forties or early fifties and of average height. He had been shot from behind. She counted three wounds, in the back and lower neck. Death would have come quickly, as any of the three shots could have been fatal. There were no marks suggesting that the body had been dragged there from somewhere else. Nor were there any signs that there had been a struggle. It seemed to her that the victim had been unaware of his danger, in any case until it was too late. She could see that he was armed; a leather holster strap protruded partially from under his pink shirt and there was the bulge of a pistol or revolver.

She got up and took a further look around. The corridor ahead was partially blocked by a temporary plasterboard partition, placed perhaps ten or twelve metres away from where she stood. There was a gap in the partition, and she went over to have a quick look, but there was nothing beyond except a large, open space. It was as if the rest of the building, on that floor as elsewhere, was still unfinished. The only door apart from the one leading from the stairwell was the open door close by on her right, the one where her two colleagues had just entered. She followed them into the apartment.

She immediately arrived in a large, combined living and dining room, with on its further side a long glass window that gave a spectacular view across the centre of the City of Montreal. Daylight was beginning to soften, red and green lights were appearing here and there at the tops of the office buildings and hotels, and the glow of a setting sun peered out from under some clouds that were gathered beyond the western shoulder of Mount Royal. In the distance, a plane drifted dreamily across the northern part of the city on its final approach to Dorval Airport. The silence of the moment was unreal.

Carmel gave herself a few seconds to unwind, to permit the tautness in her body to ebb. She was relieved. There had been no trouble, no shots had been fired, no further signs of violence had been encountered.

A man was sitting silently on a white sofa to her right, and she turned to look at him. He was dressed in jeans and a light blue shirt that was open at the collar. He looked pale and ran his fingers nervously through his light brown hair. "Was it you who called?" she asked.

2

Carmel remained at a prudent distance as the man dropped his hand and pushed down on an arm of the sofa, rising uncertainly to his feet. It was as if he was awakening from sleep, or seeking his balance after a bad fall. He looked at her apprehensively. "Yes. I was the one who called."

She took an appraising look at him. He was about six feet tall, of medium build, white, in his forties, and had no apparent distinguishing features, such as eyeglasses, earrings, or tattoos. All of this, she noted at a glance, automatically, without thinking. "What is your name, please?"

"Richard Seaton."

"Age?"

"Forty-four."

"Married?"

He shook his head. "No."

The other two policemen had reappeared through a doorway. "Nothing, Carmel," Charles Gagné reported. "The place is empty."

Carmel nodded and pulled out her cellphone. "Check

out the rest of the floor," she told Charles, pointing in the direction of the hallway.

She quickly placed a call back to the station. "That you, Sonny?" There was a pause. "Yes. We're OK. There's one body. Dead. Plus the guy who called. Nobody else." There was another pause. "Yes, Sonny. Of course!"

Putting the phone back into her pocket, she turned to the man standing by the sofa. "Richard?" she asked, wanting to make sure that she had the name correctly. He looked at her cautiously and gave a slight nod. "Richard. Just sit down and relax. We have to wait here until the others come. After that, you'll have to come down to the police station with me, just to answer a few questions."

He started to say something, but then seemed to think the better of it. "Are you feeling alright?" she asked.

"Yes," he answered, as he sat down again. "I'm fine."

"No wounds?"

His head jerked up and he looked angrily at her. "Of course not. I wasn't even here when it happened."

"That's good. Don't worry."

"You don't think I did it, do you? I mean... If I had done it, would I have called the police? I was at the office, for Chrissake. Check, and you'll see."

She smiled to reassure him. "I understand."

He started to calm down, and she had a closer look at him. His eyes were brown and set well apart under straight eyebrows that were fine, not bushy. He had a broad forehead, without noticeable wrinkles, and a well-defined nose that ended in a fleshy little lump at the bottom. His complexion was fresh, and the cheeks were salient and clean-shaven. The lips were thin. He definitely looked Anglo, Carmel thought, not Québecois. His was a face to be seen in downtown Montreal, where all the big offices were located, or in Westmount, where wealthy people lived in their fine old stone houses with slate roofs and stone steps that led up to a front door set between wrought-iron railings.

Undoubtedly, he was upset, but he didn't seem nervous. Stunned, rather. She looked closely at his hands. They weren't trembling. Nor was he openly sweating. There were no outward signs that he might have been the murderer, no traces of blood on his clothes, no clothes torn or buttons missing. Carmel was aware that her observations at this point in time were crucial. She could evaluate Richard whilst he was still subject to the emotions of the moment. It was always an advantage to be the first to arrive at the scene of a crime. Your perceptions were as close to the event as possible, and for that reason they were particularly acute.

"You knew him?" She pointed in the direction of the body that was lying outside in the hall.

"Yes." There was a long silence, during which he seemed to be holding himself together in order to master his emotions. He then let out his breath with a strange sobbing noise. "Yes. He was my half-brother."

"Your half-brother! Were you close?"

He thought a while before replying. "Sort of. We were close when we were young. Then he left home and we lost sight of each other."

"A half-brother, you say?"

"Yes. We had the same mother, but our fathers were different." He twisted his hands together and repeated himself. "We had the same mother. She was close to both of us. She would be devastated if she could see him now. Poor Carlos! It's terrible. Just terrible."

Carmel gave him a moment to recover. She was surprised that the dead man had a Spanish name. "You called him Carlos. That was his name?"

"Yes. Carlos. Carlos Antana."

"Carlos Antana," she repeated. She said nothing further, waiting for Richard to continue.

He looked up at Carmel. "May I go see him again?" he asked.

Carmel thought quickly, and decided it would be safe, as long as she stayed close by. She didn't want Richard to do anything foolish. "Yes. Of course. But please don't touch anything."

He rose and went out into the corridor. She followed quietly behind, at a respectful distance. For several minutes, he stood by the twisted corpse, looking down at it, crying silently. He had a white handkerchief in one hand, and frequently raised it to his face, or blew his nose. They finally returned to the sofa in the living room. "If I had come earlier, perhaps..." he started to say as he sat down once more and buried his face in his hands.

Carmel agreed. "You never know."

Richard looked at his hands. "I was starting to enjoy seeing him again. We were getting caught up, remembering things together. It's too late now. Why is it that we don't spend more time with others before it's too late?"

"I understand," Carmel said. "Believe me, I do."

Gagné and Perras had reappeared, and Carmel asked them to stay with Richard while she had a look around, herself.

There was not much to see. The apartment was sparsely furnished and without decoration. There were two bedrooms with queen-size double beds, each with their own bathroom. There was also a kitchenette, and one or two closets. Both bedrooms showed signs of having been occupied. As for the rest of the floor, it was just a big empty space, with nice views of Verdun, as Charles had said half-jokingly when he returned from his own inspection.

Carmel noted that the body was in view of both the door of the apartment and the opening in the partition out in the hall, only that in the first case it was five or six metres away, whilst the distance from the opening in the partition was somewhat greater, perhaps twice as much. It seemed plausible that the shots had been fired from either the apartment door or the gap in the partition. It was also possible that they had been fired by someone who came up in the elevator with the victim and then followed him out of the elevator and into the hall.

When she returned, Richard leaned forward on the sofa and looked anxiously at his watch. "How long do we have to stay here? Am I under some form of arrest?"

Carmel smiled, wanting to reassure him. "No, but you can't go just now. You're a material witness, and we need to ask you a few questions. That's all. Don't be alarmed. Nobody is saying that you did it."

Richard settled back on the sofa. "I'll cooperate, don't worry. If only for his sake." He gestured towards the door.

"Where had he been living?"

"In the Bahamas."

"And then he came here, to Montreal. Was it to see you?"

"That, I think, and other things. We were able to see each other two or three times over the last week."

"Here? Had he been staying here?"

"Yes."

"Alone?"

"No. With two or three others."

"Travelling as a group? Also from the Bahamas?"

"I guess so."

"What brought you here just now? When you arrived, your half-brother was already dead."

The directness of her question seemed to give him a

jolt. "Someone called me, about an hour ago. She told me to come."

"Who called? Did you know who it was?"

"Yes. My half-brother's companion, or chauffeur, or I don't know what. A woman called Gloria."

"His mistress, maybe?"

Richard seemed surprised. "I hadn't thought of that," he admitted.

"Anyway, we know her name is Gloria. Did she call from here?"

"No. She must have been outside on a street somewhere. I could hear traffic." Richard started to cough.

"Are you sure you're alright? Your clothes look damp."

"Oh, I'm fine thanks. It's just that I got caught in that rain shower when I arrived." He looked at his watch again. "I'm supposed to be playing squash with a friend at seven. Can I call him?"

"Just send him a text message. Tell him you can't make it."

He pulled out his cellphone and tapped a quick message, before looking back at Carmel. "You know, life is strange. If I hadn't received that phone call, I wouldn't have come here in the first place. I wouldn't be here with you now. I wouldn't even be aware that Carlos had been shot."

She shrugged. "Perhaps. But after all, he was your half-brother. Sooner or later, you would have become involved. Some things are inevitable, Richard. It's just the how and the when that vary."

Carmel raised her head and glanced out into the hallway. The others had arrived, two men and a woman, dressed in white uniforms and lugging heavy cases. The woman had a medical kit with her. She had put on a mask and white latex gloves and was in the process of kneeling down beside the body. The men carried cameras and were making a careful record of everything that was there, starting with the body and the hallway.

"We can go now, Richard," Carmel said.

He rose to his feet and looked about. For a moment, he paused, as though in prayer. Carmel then led the way out of the room, walking with a sure step. Richard followed behind, and Gagné and Perras brought up the rear.

3

Sonny rose from behind his desk and stretched out a hand to Richard. "Thanks for calling us, and for coming in to help. I'm Sonny Samuels. I do homicides." He said this casually, as if he was an interior decorator who did curtains, or an artist who did seascapes.

"Hello," Richard replied cautiously. He shook Sonny's hand and turned to give an anxious look towards Carmel. She had gone over to one of the two chairs and was standing there, waiting for the others to sit down.

Carmel didn't like Sonny's office. Its walls were an uninspiring shade of green. She had once even suggested that he have the room repainted, only to be informed that it was his wife who had chosen the colour. She retreated at once. It wouldn't do for her to cross swords with Mrs Samuels!

There were also several diplomas and testimonials on the walls with heavy black frames, things that Carmel would have left at home unpacked in a cardboard box. The rest of Sonny's office was City of Montreal standard issue—chairs and a desk of stainless steel, with their surfaces in a grey synthetic material, and a clock on the wall that now showed that it was ten past seven.

Sonny himself wore a dark suit and white shirt open at the collar. It was his uniform. He had an easygoing face with a small, bushy moustache. His hair had once been black, but now was a silver grey. He had brown eyes that seemed inherently kind, but at the same time, one could read into them the look of the public servant who was both tired and disillusioned. "Perhaps you could tell me..." Richard started.

Sonny interrupted him with a quick smile and a wave of the hand. "I know how you must feel. Please sit down. Just a few questions, a little chat, that's all. Don't worry, we'll be as brief as we can. Then we'll let you go." His assistant had entered the room with three glasses of water. "Or would you prefer coffee?" Sonny asked. Richard shook his head. Water would be fine, he said.

The two men sat down facing each other across the desk. Carmel took the chair that was off to one side. She was holding a pad and a long pencil and preparing to take notes. This was the way she and Sonny liked to do interviews. One would ask the questions, while the other observed and took notes.

"Your name and occupation?" Sonny enquired.

"Richard James Seaton." He paused. "I'm an engineer."

"You've had a nasty experience," Sonny continued. "I gather you were related to the victim. My condolences."

Richard stared evenly at him. "Thank you."

"Firstly, please understand that this is voluntary on your part. If you don't want to help us at this time, or if you want to call your lawyer, just say so."

"No thanks. I'm fine. I have nothing to hide." Richard fiddled for a while with his hands and ended up holding them together in his lap. "Where do you want me to start?"

"Tell me a bit about the victim."

Richard spoke slowly, with deliberation. "His name was Carlos Antana. He was born to my mother in her teens, and just who his father was, no one seems to know. When she was still very young, my mother went on a school trip to South America and came back pregnant. My grandparents agreed that she should keep the baby, and they called him Carlos. Later on, my mother met and married my father, and shortly after that, I was born. So you see, he and I were half-brothers. We had the same mother, but not the same father."

Carmel scribbled furiously. She hoped Richard's answers would become more spontaneous, and a little less long. Sonny nodded silently, encouraging Richard to continue.

"Carlos lived with us until he was seventeen or eighteen. When he left home, I was about eleven."

"So he was about seven years older than you."

"About that, yes. I'm forty-four. He would be fifty-one or fifty-two."

"Were you sad when he left home?"

Richard appeared surprised by Sonny's question. "Sad? I guess so. It must have left a hole, as we had no other brothers or sisters. It's pretty hard to remember how you may have felt that long ago."

Carmel could only agree, but she knew what Sonny was doing. He was asking indirect questions, ones that would make Richard talk, ones that couldn't have an obvious answer. He wasn't trying to learn everything, from start to finish. Rather, he was looking for background information, little things that might give an idea of who the dead man was, what his relationships were with the others around him, who might have wished to murder him. Above all, he was sizing Richard up. Was he a suspect? Was his information reliable? Could he have a motive for wishing his half-brother dead? After the first interview, there would be plenty of other opportunities to learn more, to fill in the gaps.

Sonny nodded. "Where did he go? Where did your half-brother go when he left home?"

"South America, somewhere. We never heard from him, though. Or very little, in any event."

"No letters? No requests for money?"

Richard almost smiled. "Not that I was aware of."

"And then?"

"The only time I saw him after that was when our mother died." He pursed his lips. "That would be ten years ago. Carlos came for the funeral and then disappeared again."

Sonny looked at him closely. "Are you saying that since he left home, when you were eleven years old, you only met or heard from him once, until now? That one time being your mother's funeral, about ten years ago?"

"Yes. That's right."

"Then, this week he contacted you."

"Yes. It was last Sunday. I had been up north on a fishing trip, and when I got home, I found a flyer under my front door advertising some sort of a show."

"Excuse me. Where's home? Where do you live?"

"Near Westmount Park. I have an apartment there. I live alone."

"Thanks. So you say you found a flyer under your door."

"Yes I did, advertising the show. On it was written by hand, in big letters, 'Come, Richard. There will be two tickets waiting for you at the door. Your brother, Carlos.' From the flyer, I could see that his full name was Carlos Antana. Otherwise, I wouldn't have known what it was.

While he was at home with us, he was Carlos Seaton."

"Last Sunday, you say. Just four days ago."

"That's right."

"And did you go to the show?"

"Yes, I did. Naturally, I was very surprised to hear from him. At the same time, I was intrigued. What was he up to? What was this show all about? So, yes, I went to the show."

"When was it?"

"It was the next evening, last Monday. I saw him out there, in the show, but that night, we never met, we never spoke to each other."

"Was it well attended?"

"The show? Well…so-so. Maybe six or eight hundred people in the stands. Something like that."

"You say that he was on stage as well."

"Yes, but there was no stage. It all happened out on the floor of a hockey arena."

Sonny played silently with his moustache, his eyes half shut. Then he turned to Richard once more. "What was your half-brother's involvement with shows and with acting, do you know?"

"Yes, I do. He loved acting. He was a natural comic. There were times, when he was still living at home, that he had us all in stitches. Mum and me in particular. I don't think my father approved."

"Tell me more about the show."

Richard shook his head slowly and suppressed an embarrassed laugh. "It lasted forty minutes, perhaps an hour, and involved a lot of people doing strange things out there in front of us. There was loud music, plenty of lighting effects, and I guess you would call them 'happenings'. There was no plot." Carmel sensed that the show hadn't been much to Richard's liking.

"Happenings?" Sonny asked. "What do you mean by that?"

"Frankly, they were a bit ridiculous. Like I said, there were people all over the place, doing funny things. In one spot, a guy—he was an older gent, and wore a cowboy hat—he set up an ironing board, took off his pants and pressed them. Somewhere else, a man dressed in a business suit with a bright red necktie led out a cow and started milking her. Just in front of us, a man pranced about with a big cardboard roulette wheel over his head, wearing nothing else but a pair of black boxer shorts. Things like that."

Carmel looked down at her note pad and suppressed a laugh. "Not something for Mrs Samuels," she thought.

"At the end, a man came out and made a sort of grand procession amongst the actors. I had a good look. It had to be him. It had to be my half-brother Carlos. He was dressed in bright colours, and the loud music and the spotlights made the whole thing seem pretty spectacular."

"What was your reaction to seeing him?" Both Sonny and Carmel watched Richard's face closely.

His eyes glistened. "Even though I thought the show was absurd, I sort of felt proud of him. He was doing his thing. His presence out there was important to him, was something that he wanted to do."

"Did you meet up with him after the show?"

"No. We waited for him outside, but he didn't show up."

"We?"

"Yes. I was with a friend."

Footsteps echoed briefly in the corridor outside. Carmel glanced at her watch. That would be Charles Gagné, returning from his supper.

Sonny continued with his questions. "You went to the show with someone else, you said."

"Yes. Someone I met when I was fishing in Labrador. A woman called Emma. She was down in Montreal, visiting a friend."

"Do you know each other well?"

"No. We met for the first time when I was up fishing. She's a fishing guide. She worked at the place where I was staying."

"What did she think of the show?"

"She didn't like it very much. She said it had almost no female actors, just men. I think she's a bit of a feminist." He gave a rapid smile. "I don't mean that in the derogatory sense, of course."

Carmel shot a curious glance over at Sonny, who simply nodded. "No. Of course not. So when did you finally meet Carlos?"

"The following morning. That would be just two days ago."

"What happened?"

"That morning, I went to the office a bit later than usual..."

Sonny interrupted him. "Excuse me. Where do you work?"

"John Bechstein and Associates. We're consulting engineers." He looked at Sonny expectantly. "Do you want the address?"

Sonny waved a hand. "No. Not now, thanks."

"At eleven or so," Richard continued. "No. It must have been later than that. Anyway, I received a call from the girl at reception. She said I had a visitor. I went out to reception, and standing there smelling of whisky and eau de cologne was my half-brother Carlos."

"You recognised him?"

"Of course. After all, I had seen him in the show the previous night."

"True enough. Had he been drinking, do you think?"

"No. But he was certainly hung over."

"What happened next?"

"He hugged me and made quite a scene, telling me how happy he was to see me after all the years that had gone by. I led him back to my office as quickly as possible. I found the way he appeared slightly embarrassing."

"All the same, were you happy to see him again?"

"For sure." Richard nodded his head emphatically. "Yes, really. At the same time, I was surprised. I hadn't expected him to show up like that, right out of the blue."

"Did he seem to be in good health?"

"I guess so, for his age. When we arrived at my office, he was out of breath. He looked about and, seeing a plant I have growing in a big pot in the corner, he complained. He said that the plant was sucking all the oxygen out of the air. I found that pretty ridiculous, but I think that he liked saying strange things like that."

That would be the actor in him, Carmel thought. She was starting to form a portrait of the dead man in her mind. He must have been an interesting character.

"We started to discuss old times, and he seemed anxious to re-establish the relationship between us, to reclaim me as his brother." Richard was smiling now. "He talked about the house near the centre of Montreal where we were brought up in the 1980s—the blue Plymouth, our model airplanes, the neighbour's cat. He even brought up the first day I went to school, how he had to drag me up the steps after I burst into tears and demanded to return home."

It was Carmel's turn to smile, if only to herself. Her younger brother Marcel had been like that when she took him for his first day at primary school, in the little village next to their farm.

Richard continued. "Carlos had a surprising memory for all these things, but of course, he was quite a bit older than me when we were both living at home together."

"What else did you discuss?"

"At one point, our conversation turned to my father, and he became quite angry. He told me how it had been my father who had more or less forced him to leave home when he did."

"He said that?"

"Yes. I think Carlos must have suffered from the fact that he wasn't my father's son, that he was born an illegitimate child, that my father didn't treat him the same as he treated me."

"You already said that your father didn't appreciate the comic side of his personality."

"That's correct. They had rows. My father was very hard on him."

"How had your half-brother been living more recently? Did he tell you?"

"He lived in Nassau, in the Bahamas. He told me about a night club that he owns—well owned, now, I guess—in Nassau together with his business partner, a man named Rupert Marsham, and about the shows that they had put on together."

"How long did his visit to your office last?" Carmel asked.

Richard turned towards her. "Half an hour, perhaps. Not much more."

"Did the two of you argue?" Sonny asked. "Were there any differences of opinion?"

"No. None at all."

"What did you think when he left your office? Why do you think he came to see you?"

"That was the mystery of it all. He came, we talked,

and then he left. He didn't ask for anything. It was as if he wanted to look me over, to see what I was like."

Richard reached for his glass and had a long drink of water. Carmel looked up from her notepad and studied his face. So far, he hadn't contradicted himself, or given any reason for them to think that he was making it up, or that he had something to hide. He was an interesting person, however. So, it seemed, had been Carlos. She was beginning to look forward to getting her teeth into the file and hoped that Sonny would agree that she take charge of the investigation.

Sonny waited for Richard to put his glass down, and then continued. "Then what happened?"

"He just left. I worked straight through lunch, finished early, and went for a game of squash with a friend called Freddy. Afterwards, Freddy and I went down to a place on Bleury where we sometimes go for a few drinks and a bite to eat."

"And did you see your half-brother again, before today?"

"Yes, I did. The next day was a Wednesday, yesterday in fact, the day when I usually stay home for an hour or two in the morning to do a bit of housekeeping. After an early lunch, I went to the office and took my messages. There was one from Carlos, but I didn't answer it right away because I had to sign off on some plans for a radar site in Turkey."

"That's the sort of work you do, radar sites?"

Richard looked up. "Yes. I'm an electrical engineer. My specialty is communications systems, radar for civil and military applications, satellite communications... that sort of thing." Sonny nodded appreciatively. "I have special clearance from the RCMP to do defence work for the Government of Canada," Richard added, with a hint of pride. No doubt he felt that being vetted by the Mounties was a further guarantee of his innocence.

"So there was a message from your half-brother asking you to call him," Sonny continued. "Did you do so?"

"Yes. I did. It was a woman who answered. She asked me who was calling, and when I told her, she got quite excited, calling out, 'Carlos. It's Richard! Come quickly.' The next moment, Carlos was there on the line. He was almost shouting. He said that he had been so happy to see me again, asked me where I was, what I was doing. It went on like that for a while, and he finally insisted that I join them for a drink and a bite of supper. He told me that his assistant, whose name was Gloria, would be around with a car to pick me up outside my office in half an hour."

"And you accepted?"

"Well, yes. I was happy to see him again."

Carmel leaned forward in her chair. "Excuse me. This would have been at about what time?"

"Four-thirty. Maybe five." He reached for his glass and took another sip of water. "When I went down to the sidewalk in front of the building where I work, a long white Mercedes had pulled up, and its driver was standing beside the passenger door, ready to open it for me. 'Hello, Richard,' she said. 'I'm Gloria.'"

Sonny looked up at Richard. "Tell me about her."

"Mid-thirties. Stylishly dressed. Really beautiful. There aren't many like her."

"And her name is Gloria," Carmel said. "That sounds appropriate!" She wondered if it was her real name.

"Yes. She also had a glorious bruise under her left eye."

"What kind of bruise?" Carmel asked, surprised.

"A black eye. A shiner. The kind you get when somebody hits you."

Carmel's curiosity was aroused. She realised that this was also the woman Richard said had called him and told him to go down to the condo, on the afternoon of the murder. "Describe her a bit more. What colour is her hair?"

"Golden red. Halfway down the back."

"Her last name?" Sonny enquired.

"Marsham. Gloria Marsham. She's married, to the man I mentioned, to Rupert Marsham."

"Rupert Marsham. That's the former business partner?"

"Yes."

"So she drove you off in her car."

"Yes. It took us about ten minutes. It was a beautiful, sunny afternoon. We drove down Park Avenue, and I felt quite important in that white limousine, driven by a beautiful woman. I was sitting beside her, of course, not behind. We reached the apartment building, the one where I found the body this afternoon, and Gloria drove us down into the garage. She parked the car and we went up in the elevator. When we reached the top floor, where the condo was, the door opened, and there, waiting to greet me, stood Carlos."

"How did he look?"

Richard swallowed hard. "He looked spectacular. He was wearing some sort of a white robe that could have been Roman, or Emirati, or God only knows what. Behind him, through the big picture window, I could see Mount Royal. It was all pretty dramatic. 'Bless you for coming, Richard,' he said, and gave me a big hug."

They waited for a moment while Richard had another sip of water.

"We sat down on one of the white sofas by the window. Everything was white up there, his robe, the curtains, the upholstery, even the carpets. He had a pinkish look to his face, as though he had put on a bit of makeup. He was wearing a large gold ring on one finger, and several gold chains around his neck.”

Carmel frowned. She hadn't seen any gold ring or chains on the corpse. She supposed that the victim must have dressed up for that last evening with his half-brother. She wondered who had the gold chains now.

“What did you discuss?”

“We discussed the show, and he asked me about the friend I had with me. When I told him, he said that she sounded very nice, and that he intended to go up to Labrador himself some time, as he had a foster son living there.”

“I asked him if his show had made a profit, and he sighed and explained that Montreal audiences weren't used to shows like his, that the gate had been less than expected, and that there had been a number of additional expenses. Gloria arrived at this point with a bottle of Champagne and some glasses and laughed. ‘Carlos, darling,’ she said. ‘Your shows never make money, let's face it.’ She put the Champagne down on a table and wrapped her arms around him.”

“Was he surprised? How did he react?”

“To her hugging him? He certainly didn't discourage it!”

Carmel smiled to herself. The image of a classic triangle was forming in her mind—Carlos, Rupert, Gloria...

Sonny didn't react. “And then?”

“And then,” Richard continued, “he started to ask me what I did with my time, was I married, all of that. I filled him in and told him that I was living on the ground floor of a house in Lower Westmount, and that the apartment above me belonged to an older woman who kept cats. He asked if she was an engineer as well. 'No,' I told him. 'She's an accountant. A tax accountant.'"

"For some reason, this got him quite excited. He stood up, and grabbing the Champagne bottle, pulled off the wire fastener. 'I have a very good accountant in Nassau,' he said. 'She has me all set up, Panama companies, bearer shares, all of that. You should see my corporate chart! I call it my two-tiered tandem sidestep.' He started dancing a little jig, there, in front of the table. I was afraid the Champagne bottle would burst, the way he was waving it around. The three of us were laughing now, and Gloria took the bottle of Champagne from him, opened it, and poured us each a glass. Carlos then proposed a toast. It was a toast to us, to the brothers."

"An emotional moment."

"Yes, it was. We made small talk for a while longer, then a side door opened and a tall, stooped man with bushy black hair stood there. Age about forty, maybe a bit more. He didn't even look at me, but turned to Gloria and said, 'Get out! Get out, you.' Like she was a dog, or something."

Sonny looked over at Carmel. The bad guy in the piece! "That must have poured cold water on your celebration!"

"It sure did. I was surprised, to say the least, and looked at Carlos, then at Gloria. 'Rupert,' Carlos said calmly. 'This is my brother, Richard. Richard, please meet my business partner, Rupert Marsham.'"

"This man Rupert was still looking at Gloria, who glared at him, but slowly got up and left the room. Rupert waited until she had closed the door behind her. 'Twenty-six thousand,' he said to Carlos. 'A bit more, but not much. Pretty disappointing.'"

"You think they were talking about the take from the show?"

"I'm certain they were. Carlos asked how they should

split it. He suggested they each take a third. Rupert was very rude. He said he wanted twenty thousand, and that Carlos could split the rest any way he wanted."

"So Carlos felt that the three of them were instrumental in putting on the show?"

"Yes. I guess so. Somehow, the awkwardness passed, and we sat down for some pizza, the four of us. Gloria put it on the table, together with a bottle of red wine. The conversation dragged, Carlos seemed deflated by Rupert's behaviour, and Gloria just sulked."

"Not much fun," Sonny prompted.

"No, it was sort of unpleasant. At one point, Rupert said that their flights were all organised for the following night, and that Carlos had better be ready."

Sonny looked rapidly at Carmel. "I see. Where do you think they were flying to?"

"Back to the Bahamas, I imagine."

Sonny stretched. "Richard. Let's take five. What do you think? You have been very helpful, very cooperative. A break will do us all good. Then we'll talk again for a short while, and we can let you go."

Richard didn't protest. Carmel could see that he was too exhausted to resist. He probably just wanted to finish up and go home.

4

Once she had led Richard out of the room, Carmel returned for a little talk with Sonny. "What's your view so far?" he asked her.

"He's OK. I'd say he's telling the truth. He doesn't seem to me to be at all complex, or dishonest. When I first saw him at the condo, he was reasonably calm, and his reactions were pretty normal. It's the same now."

"I think you're right. I think that he's telling the truth. The problem may be in the things he forgets to tell us."

"Or is reluctant to tell us. Get him to say a bit more about the woman he went to the show with. And the other one as well, the one with the black eye."

Sonny looked at her with a laugh. "You always suspect the women. It seems to be a part of your psychological makeup."

She shook her head in protest. "I just understand them better than you do. You put women on a pedestal, Sonny. You never suspect them. With you, they fly under the radar."

"Under the radar?" Sonny laughed. "I wish!" He

straightened up in his chair. "Carmel. Could you please get Gagné to check tonight's flights to the Bahamas, probably through Toronto? While you're doing that, I'll notify Admin that we want a news blackout for at least two days. Then we can finish up with Richard."

She nodded. She liked working with Sonny. They made a good team. This was his twentieth year in the force, and nominally, he was her superior. However, when it came to an actual case, they were equals.

Richard was sitting outside in the reception area when Carmel went back to fetch him. He looked pretty limp. "How am I doing?" he asked her with the hint of a smile. "This is worse than going to the dentist's."

"Just fine," she reassured him. "You're doing fine. A few more questions and we'll let you go."

They went back into Sonny's office.

Sonny resumed where they had left off. "You were telling us about your visit to the apartment yesterday evening."

"Yes, I was. At about eight o'clock, Gloria offered to drive me home, and the two of us left together. Once we were in the car, she apologised to me for her husband's behaviour. I commented that he seemed to have quite a hold over Carlos. She said that they generally got on well together, but that when it came to money, her husband could get a bit vicious. She added that they were all going to meet the next afternoon to divide the take from the show, and that it might get tricky. Those were her very words."

"In other words, they were going to divide the money this afternoon, and then take a flight back to the Bahamas?"

"That was my understanding."

"So the three of them were travelling together. Is that right?"

"Do you mean Carlos, Rupert and Gloria? Yes. That was how it looked to me."

"Had all three been living in the apartment?"

"I can't say for sure, but I would say so, yes."

"Was anyone else staying there with them? People connected with the show, for example."

"The only other person I am aware of is a man named Todd, whom I met briefly this morning, but I don't think he was staying in the apartment.

Sonny looked over at Carmel, waiting for her to finish writing. "So what happened today?" He asked this with a pleasant smile, as though Richard was about to tell him about a trip to the zoo.

"At nine-fifteen this morning, I left the house and started to walk to work. When I reached Atwater, my cellphone rang. Gloria was on the line. She said that Carlos wanted to see me one last time before he left and asked me where I was. I told her that I was walking along Sherbrooke Street."

"They were nearby in the car, on their way to buy some office supplies to take back to Nassau, and she offered to give me a lift. She said I should go to the corner of Guy and wait for them there. I was happy to think that I would see Carlos again, so I kept on going, and when I reached the corner of Guy, I stopped and looked around. Sure enough, the white Mercedes appeared out of the traffic, with Gloria at the wheel. She gave me a big smile and waved for me to get in."

"Carlos was seated in the back with another man whom I didn't recognise, so I sat in front beside Gloria. Carlos leaned forward in his seat—he was sitting just behind me—and said a few words. He then introduced me to the man beside him, the one I had never seen before. He gave his name. It was a single name. Todd."

Carmel intervened. "Describe him for us, could you?"

"Middle-aged and balding. He wore a summer-weight business suit. Steel-rimmed glasses." Richard made a face and shrugged. "Kind of ordinary looking, I guess."

Sonny stroked his moustache. "Did he have a presence? Did he seem important? What vibes did he give off?"

"He seemed important, yes, but personally, I didn't like him at all."

"Why not?"

"I don't know. He seemed slippery, if you know what I mean."

"What happened next?"

"Carlos explained that Todd was one of his important financial backers. Todd and I shook hands, and that was about all."

"Short and sweet."

"Yes, short and sweet. In no time at all, we reached my office. I jumped out of the car. Carlos lowered his window, and we shook hands. I waved goodbye to the others."

"And that was it?"

"Yes. That is to say, until this afternoon."

"Of course. Before we start with that, though, what was your impression after you left the car? Why did Carlos want to see you again?"

Richard thought for a while. "Presumably, he wanted to introduce me to the man called Todd. Perhaps he thought that something might happen to him, something not very nice, and that in that case, Todd could contact me. I just don't know."

"But you're saying that now, with the knowledge that something not very nice did happen to Carlos. What did you think, then?"

"I guess I was puzzled. If anything, I was thinking

that this was the last time I would be seeing Carlos for a while, that it had been great seeing him again, that we would somehow have to stay in contact, things like that.”

“OK. Let’s hear about this afternoon.”

Richard spoke with precision. “Once I reached my office, I made a few phone calls and had a talk with one or two colleagues. Shortly after twelve, I went to the little coffee shop in the basement of our building and had a sandwich. Back upstairs some forty minutes later, I signed off on some drawings for a communications tower and made one or two phone calls. At about three-thirty, my secretary came into my office to tell me that she wanted to leave early to have her nails done. I let her go.”

He paused. “Shortly after that, our receptionist buzzed me to say that someone was calling and wanted to talk to me urgently. I took the call. It was Gloria. She must have been calling from outdoors somewhere, because I could hear cars going by. To the best of my memory, her words were as follows. ‘Richard, come quickly. To the condo. Please, for Carlos’ sake. Hurry.’ She hung up immediately.”

“I felt that I had no choice but to go; it sounded that urgent. I cleaned up my desk, left the building, hailed a taxi, and gave the driver the address of the condo. The traffic was terrible, and it suddenly started to rain just as I arrived. I took the stairs up to the condo, because the elevator wasn’t working, arrived in the hallway outside the condo, and it was there that I found Carlos.”

“Dead?”

Richard leaned back in his chair, struggling to get the word out. “Yes.”

“Very sad,” Sonny murmured, half to himself. He stared at the ceiling for a good half minute, and the room remained silent. Finally, he turned to Richard again. “I’m very sorry. About your half-brother, I mean. He seems to have been an interesting person. Tell me, Richard, were there any noises or signs of other people upstairs, where you found the body?"

"No. I looked around to see if there was anyone, then I went into the condo, sat on the sofa, called the police, and didn't move from there until they had arrived."

"Did you see any unusual objects—like a weapon, like money, like clothing, anything of the sort in the stairwell, in the hallway, or in the condo itself?"

"No."

"Is there anything else you think you should tell us at this time?"

Richard thought for a while. "No, not really."

Carmel leaned forward. "When Gloria called you the second time, to tell you to go to the condo, did she sound frightened, or anxious perhaps, or did she sound calm?"

Richard thought for a while. "She sounded more anxious than calm."

"What about when you saw her this morning? When they gave you that lift. How did she seem?"

"She seemed alright. Calm, I guess. In fact, when I got out of the car, I forgot my laptop, and she called me back and gave it to me. She seemed to be laughing at me, in a friendly sort of way."

Sonny rose from his chair and gave Richard a reassuring smile. "Many thanks, Richard. You've given us a lot to think about. We can let you go now, but I'm sure that we will want to speak to you again, once we are further along in our investigation." Richard gave a visible sigh of relief.

Carmel also got up. "Sonny. I would like to ask Richard something." She turned to Richard. "Richard. I want to ask you a favour. A big favour." She paused, and

Richard remained silent. "I would like to meet Emma, just to ask her a few questions. Would you mind that? Do you think you could ask her to come see us?"

Richard's face flushed red with anger. "Emma? Why her? She has nothing to do with all of this."

Carmel wasn't surprised by his reaction. Richard struck her as being the sort of gallant male that never succeeded in treating a woman on equal terms. A bit like Sonny. She insisted. Speaking with Emma would allow her to check up on what Richard had been saying. "Just a short interview," she asked persuasively.

He sighed. "I don't like having to impose any of this on her. I really don't."

"If you don't, we can," Carmel reminded him.

Richard blinked. "Alright. I'll speak to her."

Carmel smiled her most winning smile. "Thanks, Richard. Tomorrow morning. Here. At eleven, say."

5

"Carlos seems to have surrounded himself with some pretty dangerous characters," Carmel said to Sonny, once Richard had left them.

"I hope they caught their plane," he replied. "Then we can hand the whole shebang over to the police in Nassau."

Carmel shook her head. "Don't get your hopes up, Sonny. If you ask me, we haven't seen the last of them. They came here for some reason, not just to visit the wax museum. And certainly not to keep Carlos company while he put on that show of his and looked up his long-lost half-brother."

She had caught Sonny's interest. "Oh? Why do you say that?"

"For starters, we have to decide if we can rely on what Richard has been telling us. I'm prepared to do so until events prove me wrong. Tomorrow morning's interview with Emma will give us an opportunity to check on some of the things he has been telling us. I hope you'll join me."

"Sure, if I'm free. I'll also get in touch with the police in Nassau to see if they can give us any leads. But tell me, why do you think that they may still be in Montreal?"

"It's just a hunch. Firstly, the show didn't make money. According to Gloria, they never do. So why would Rupert, who seems to love money more than anything else, why would he have come along? He must have had some other reason."

Carmel riffled through the notes she had taken. "And Carlos particularly wanted Richard to meet Todd, whom he described as an important financial backer. Reason unexplained. However, the show had already happened. Why was Todd still here?"

Sonny nodded. "You're saying that Todd remained here, and was presented to Richard, because something else was planned."

"Precisely."

"You could be right. A bank heist, or a drug shipment. What do you think of Carlos himself? He may have been an interesting eccentric, but I don't think that he was a fool."

"Certainly no fool. But he was an actor, we have to remember that. There was perhaps another side to him, behind his acting."

"And do you believe all that talk about dividing up the take from the show?"

"Yes, I think we have to. Rupert made his comments to Carlos in front of Richard, and Gloria referred to it afterwards."

"That could provide a motive."

"I suppose so. It doesn't seem to me to be an awful lot of money."

"A better motive, in Rupert's case, would be to get his hands on the half of the theatre in Nassau that Carlos still owned."

They were turning that thought over in their minds

when there were steps in the hallway outside, and Charles Gagné's head appeared at the door. "Sorry to interrupt. Just to say that there is no record of a Rupert Marsham or a Gloria Marsham being booked on a flight out of Montreal tonight."

Carmel and Sonny looked at each other, and Carmel thanked Gagné.

"Two more things, Charles, before you go home. Could you please find out at what time it started to rain in central Montreal late this afternoon? Also, please check the web to see if there is any mention of a show in a hockey arena last Monday evening, put on by someone called Carlos Antana."

"Shall do." He smiled and disappeared.

Sonny nodded approvingly. "You have him well trained!"

Carmel laughed. "He's terrific. Tomorrow, I'll ask him to locate the taxi driver who drove Richard down to the condo."

Sonny nodded his approval. "Someone should go to the office where Richard worked and ask them a few questions."

"Yes. I was going to do that tomorrow."

"Good. And how did you find Perras?"

"He was fine. Just fine. I'll get him to take Richard down to the morgue tomorrow for a formal identification of the body."

Carmel shifted in her chair and continued. "Coming back to what we have learned already, I am struck by the fact that Carlos and Gloria seemed to get along well together, whereas Rupert and Gloria do not."

"Hang on, Carmel. Didn't Richard say that Rupert and Gloria are husband and wife?"

Carmel looked sharply up at Sonny. "What about

it? If it was Rupert who gave her the black eye, and that seems likely, then he's an animal, and he's both violent and dangerous."

Sonny shrugged. "And yet, she sort of stands up for him, tells Richard later on that Rupert isn't so bad, it's just that he's a little greedy!"

Carmel thought of that for a while. "True enough."

"Rupert was pretty rude to Carlos, even if they were business partners. I wonder why Carlos put up with it. Was he soft? Or was he just biding his time?"

She paused. "Perhaps both."

"Which brings us to Todd, whom Richard clearly did not like. What's your take on him?"

"He remains a mystery, at least for now, but one thing is certain, and that is that he is somehow connected with the group. After all, Richard met him with Carlos and Gloria. I doubt he stayed in the apartment, though. There are only two beds, and he didn't join them for supper when Richard was there." They were both silently asking themselves the same question. *Whose bed did Gloria sleep in?*

"Todd, Rupert and Gloria," Sonny mused. "They make an interesting group. A faceless man in his fifties. A violent man in his forties, and a glamorous woman in her thirties. I wonder who's running the show."

"Don't you mean 'Calling the shots'?"

He laughed. "If you prefer."

"No, not really. But someone is in charge. Maybe it's Todd."

"Maybe. So you think they are still here in Montreal. We're going to have to find a way to track them down."

"I'll start with the white Mercedes. It was probably rented."

Just then, Charles Gagné reappeared at the door with

a big grin on his face. He was waving a sheet of paper in his hand, and passed it to Carmel, who had a quick look, winked at Charles, and placed it on the desk in front of Sonny.

He picked it up and swallowed hard. "What's this? An advert for the show? *Flummery and Flapdoodle.* That's the name of the show? Mother of Moses! Who in his right mind would pay fifty dollars to go see a show with a name like that?"

Carmel was laughing. "Like you said, Carlos seems to have been a bit of an original." Sonny just rolled his eyes.

Charles consulted a slip of paper that he had pulled out of his pocket. "The rain started to fall just before half past four," he announced.

Carmel nodded. "Just as Richard said. Thanks Charles. You can go now. See you tomorrow." He waved to them and left. "Sonny." Carmel resumed. "Let's talk about the murder itself. There are one or two things there that I find pretty interesting."

"Can we start with the time of the murder? Do we know more or less when he was killed?"

"I got there at about twenty past five. I'd say he'd been dead about an hour."

"And Richard came and went in the interval."

"Yes. That shower he mentioned was at four thirty. That was when he arrived in the taxi. He called the station nine minutes later."

"So Carlos was probably murdered at some time between four and four twenty."

"More or less. We'll see what the pathologist says. Sonny. I'm struck by the fact that Carlos was shot in the back. Not in the front, but in the back. From behind. Three times. In the hallway."

Sonny fingered his moustache thoughtfully. "Uh-huh."

"He can't have been expecting it. Not if he was shot in the back. And yet he was armed. He was wearing a chest holster, with a pistol of some sort in it."

"He didn't have the pistol in his hand?"

"No. It remained in the holster."

"Perhaps because he knew the killer and thought he had nothing to fear."

"Could be. I'm also struck by the fact that the body lay in the hallway. Carlos wasn't shot in the apartment. He was shot out in the hall. It is as though whoever shot him was trying to prevent something from happening. Trying to prevent Carlos from escaping from the apartment. Or perhaps the opposite. Trying to prevent him from going into the apartment. The way the body was placed, it could have been either."

"Was the door to the apartment open?"

"Yes. Wide open."

"Where do you think the shots were fired from? The door to the apartment?"

"From there, from just outside the elevator perhaps, or from an opening in a plasterboard partition further along in the hallway."

"Why would he have been shot three times?"

"That's an interesting point. I think any one of those shots could have done the trick, sooner or later. However, it seems to me that the shots weren't placed where a professional would have placed them. None of them were to the head. Their pattern is not the pattern of a professional killing."

Sonny nodded. "So now, let's talk about the phone call asking Richard to go to the apartment. What do you make of that?"

"It tells us a lot. Gloria clearly knew that something was going to happen. She may even have known who was going to murder Carlos. She must have wanted Richard to go there quickly, so as to prevent it."

Sonny shook his head. "Wait a minute, Carmel. There's another possibility. Maybe she wanted Richard to be there so that he would take the rap!"

6

"Hello," the woman said to Carmel. "I'm Emma Sinclair. Richard Seaton said I should come."

She was standing by a window in the reception area, simply dressed in jeans and a navy-blue wind jacket with a broad white zipper down the front. A mass of frizzy light brown hair was tied back in a green ribbon, revealing a pretty face with arched eyebrows, one or two freckles on the cheeks, and full lips. Her eyes were bright, but watchful. They were either grey or green, Carmel couldn't decide. Her face was tanned and without makeup, and her hands were working hands, with strong fingers and short nails.

Carmel introduced herself. She instinctively liked Emma. She seemed like a breath of fresh air, someone who was free of the artificiality that sometimes affects people living in the big city. "We can go in here," she said to her, pointing to a meeting room on her left, quickly asking the receptionist to call Sonny to see if he could join them.

The room was small, and without windows. They sat down beside each other at the corner of a small rectangular table, and Carmel gave Emma a reassuring smile as she opened her briefcase and pulled out a notepad and pencil. A moment later, Sonny appeared at the door.

He slid into a chair opposite Emma, trying to act informally and to put Emma at her ease. Carmel saw at once that his presence was a mistake. With him in the room, the atmosphere changed at once. Emma's face tightened, and her eyes became more wary, even hostile. It was too late now, however, so Carmel started the interview.

"I suppose that by now, Richard has told you about the murder of his half-brother."

Emma stared at her hands, neatly crossed on her lap. "Yes."

"I'm leading the enquiry, and so far, we know very little. I don't have much that I want to ask you, Emma, but it's terribly important for me to understand the background of the murder and to get a better image in my mind of the persons involved. Do you mind? Are you willing to help?" Emma nodded, but otherwise said nothing. "What is your family name, Emma?"

"Sinclair."

"Where do you live?"

"I live in Labrador. My home is in Makkovik, and I also have a place in North West River."

"Age?"

"Thirty-five."

"Family, marital status, occupation?"

"My parents are dead. I have no brothers or sisters. No children. I'm single."

"Occupation?" Carmel asked once more.

"I work as a fishing guide in the summer. I'm also a mechanic, and repair things, skidoos, outboard engines, chain saws, things like that."

For a while, they made small talk, and Carmel was able to learn a bit of Emma's personal history, the fact that she was originally from Saint John's, her Dad had been in the army, her Mom had been a nurse, she had a degree in teaching from Memorial University, and so on. She recounted this in monosyllables, and in a dancing, melodious accent that Carmel sometimes had difficulty following. She tended to look down at her hands while she spoke. Gradually, however, the ice melted, and a hesitant complicity took form between the two women. All the while, Sonny remained silent, as though he too felt that he shouldn't be there.

On several occasions, Emma wanted to be reassured that Richard was not a suspect. "He's not under arrest, or anything like that?" she asked.

Carmel sought to put her at ease. "No. Nothing like that. He's helping us out, that's all."

Emma told her that she had met Richard for the first time on the river, at the fishing camp. She had acted as guide for Richard and another guest for three days. It was only when she mentioned at the end of his stay that she too was on the plane to Montreal that Richard had asked for her phone number, and had later on called, to invite her to the show. She had not seen him since the night of the show, but they had agreed to have lunch together before she returned to Labrador on Sunday. Carmel could see that if there was anything going on between Emma and Richard, it was in its very early stages.

"Did Richard mention his half-brother Carlos to you up at the fishing camp?" she asked.

"No. We never talked about family, or stuff like that."

"I suppose that fishing guides are usually men."

"Yes. If you're a woman, you have to remain really separate. That's what I always do."

"Did he discuss his work with you, problems at the office, things like that?"

"No."

"Were you ever alone together?"

"No." She paused. "We were always three, him, me and Jake. That was the name of the other fisherman. Jake."

"Would you say Richard was a good fisherman?"

Emma looked up and tilted her head to one side. "Not bad for a beginner. He's strong. He's careful. He's patient."

"Did you ever see him get angry, or frustrated?"

"No."

"After the show, how did he react? What were his feelings about seeing his half-brother again?"

"He seemed happy enough. We discussed the show a bit. We stopped for a pizza, he drove me home, and that was about it."

"Did he like the show?"

Emma shook her head slowly. "No. He said it was a load of... Well. You know what I mean." Her mouth turned up slightly at the corners. It was the first time she had smiled.

"And you?"

She made a face. "Not my style." She leaned forward slightly, and Carmel could smell her lotion. "Carlos and the others. Their names meant nothing to me before now. I promise you. All this is new."

"What have you been doing this week, here in Montreal?"

"Me?" She thought for a moment. "Nothing special. Lots of window shopping. I went twice to the movies."

"May I ask you where you were yesterday afternoon?"

"Yesterday? At the movies. I went to see a film about Napoleon. At the Forum Cineplex."

"At what time?"

"I got there about two. There were trailers to start with. The movie ended a bit after five. Then I went straight home to the place where I'm staying, a friend's house in NDG."

Sonny had caught Carmel's eye and was pointing at his watch. They exchanged nods, and he rose to his feet. "Thank you, Ms Sinclair," he said to Emma. "You've been very helpful. I have to go, but in any event, I think Carmel has just about finished." He smiled at both of them and left the room.

"When did you say you go back to Labrador?" Carmel asked, as she started putting her things back into her briefcase.

"Day after tomorrow. I have to go back on the river and close up camp."

Carmel was intrigued. She found Emma interesting to talk to and was curious to know more about the kind of life she led. "What does that mean, to close up camp?"

Emma was more relaxed now, since Sonny's departure. "Oh, a bunch of little things. There's the dock down by the water. I have to winch it up the hill so the ice doesn't get it. Same thing for the boats. Then there are metal covers for all the windows and doors. I have to put them on because of the bears." She paused before continuing with her list, counting each item by pointing an index finger at the fingertips of the other hand. "Bleed the pipes, oil the generator, mop the floors, set the mouse traps. Stuff like that. You name it, I have to do it!"

"How long will it take?"

"Two or three days. In any case, I left my boat in Cartwright—that's the village down south next to the river—so I have to go back there to pick it up. Then I'll take it back up the coast to Makkovik, where I live."

"Oh! How far is that?"

"Three days, maybe." She shrugged. "Depends on the weather."

"Is it a big boat?"

"Yes, for sure. A beautiful boat. It's called Walrus."

"And you're going to take it up to Makkovik? Will you do that alone, all by yourself?"

"Yes, I'll do it alone." Emma didn't seem to think much of it. "I was alone when I brought it down from Makkovik in June."

Carmel had never in her life been north of Chicoutimi. For her, Makkovik was an unknown, but exotic, village somewhere in Canada's arctic. She had difficulty imagining what it would be like, living up there, travelling up and down the coast in a small boat. "It must be very special, where you live," she murmured.

Emma nodded her head vigorously. "Makkovik is really pretty. It's on a hill by the sea. I share a house there with an older couple, Johnny and Rose, and with their granddaughter Sarah and her husband, Josh. I'm very close to Josh. He is sort of like a brother or a son to me."

"The winters up there must be very long."

Emma shrugged her shoulders. "The winters aren't bad. We can go everywhere by skidoo. It's not winter now, though. Not yet. I still have to bring in the firewood. Then I have to shoot my moose." She gave Carmel a sly smile. "Not with a handgun. With my Dad's old army rifle. Then I'll be ready for the winter."

That seemed to make a good end to their conversation, and Carmel rose to thank Emma for coming to see her. As they stood by the door of the room, Emma made as if to place her right hand on Carmel's forearm, but held it back at the last moment. However, their eyes came in close contact. "I don't think he did it," Emma said. "I can't see him doing something like that."

7

Rupert Marsham looked anxiously down onto the street in front of the apartment building on Saint-Denis Street. Beside him stood a short man in a rumpled grey suit with a white T-shirt beneath. They made a strange couple, the one, a tall, gangly, dark-haired man with an angular face and close-set eyes, the other, a stocky, muscular man with a sour face and a military bearing. The second man's name was Valery, and he was Russian. That was about all that Rupert had been told about him.

"Where's Gloria?" Rupert asked himself, checking his watch. It was four in the afternoon. Down below, the Friday afternoon traffic was beginning to gather. People were heading home, or out to their cottages in the country for the weekend. "Damn that woman, anyway. She comes and she goes. You never know what she's up to."

His companion said nothing, but gestured with his hand, as if to raise a glass. "*Pivo*," he suggested in a guttural voice. "Beer."

Rupert nodded and went to fetch two cans of Bud Light. Back at the window, he handed one can to Valery and opened the other for himself. "Where are they?" he asked again.

Everything seemed to have gone according to plan the previous afternoon; at least there was that. Gloria had called him from a public phone early in the evening to say that she was going to wait until the next day before returning to the apartment on Saint-Denis Street. That made sense. There were too many persons involved, and Rupert didn't like that. He was essentially a loner. The smaller the number of people involved, the less the chance of someone screwing up.

"She's too damn independent," he explained to Valery. "She could at least have called me today, the bitch! I'll speak to her when she does get back. I should never have married her," he added.

Valery shrugged. "Why did you?" He spoke in a halting English.

"It was her idea. As far as I was concerned, we could have just kept sleeping together. I could have continued supporting her, giving her money, and that would have suited me just fine."

Valery shrugged again. "Yes. Better that way."

"She insisted. She wanted the status, she wanted the passport, she wanted the security. She also wanted my name, to call herself Gloria Marsham, rather than Gloria something-or-other." In fact, Rupert could no longer remember Gloria's maiden name.

The strident wail of a siren suddenly rose from the street below. They both peered anxiously out the window. It was just an ambulance, heading down the hill towards a nearby hospital. "Calm down," Rupert said to himself. "You've got the jitters."

They both took long swigs of beer. "A chapter of my life," Rupert said. "I have just finished a chapter of my life." He burped noisily.

Valery was puzzled. "Chapter?" he asked.

Rupert glanced at him with distaste. "Me and Carlos." He wiped the froth off his lips with a sleeve. "We've been together ten years now. When I first met him, he had just come back from serving time in a prison in Barranquilla. For what, I never learned. It can't have been serious. He wasn't there for very long. Justice in Colombia is pretty chancy."

Valery nodded in agreement and took a long drink. "Then what?"

"Carlos put on his first show, in a rented hall in Nassau. I was hired to manage things at the door, to act as bouncer. The show went well, and the owner of the building, a widow, fell for Carlos, kicked the bucket, and left the building to Carlos in her will. Typical Carlos," he said. "Always bloody lucky."

"Until now," Valery observed.

"Until now," Rupert agreed. "We opened a nightclub in the building. The Blue Angel, we called it. It became famous, the hottest place in Nassau. It was wild. Carlos kept thinking up shows to put on, with himself in the main role. He was good at that. But we made the real money at the bar. Every chick in town came to our bar. It smelled like a flower garden."

Valery raised his can of beer in a toast, and emptied it, saying something long and unpronounceable. "Cheers," Rupert replied. A collection of empties was accumulating on the table. They added theirs, and Rupert went to get two more cans in the fridge.

"One of the clients at the Club," he continued when he had returned, "was a big name in Nassau. I got to know him well. We did deals together, soft drugs, that sort of thing. He took me aside one night and gave me a box. About the size of a shoe box. 'I dig you, man,' he said. 'You're my coolest friend.' I opened the box and it was full of bundles of banknotes. American dollars. Twenties, fifties and hundreds. I asked him what he wanted me to do with them. He told me to buy a one-half share in the Blue Angel. For myself. I spoke to Carlos, and he went along with it. Now, we own the Club fifty-fifty. Except that now, Carlos is dead."

"So, you are lucky too," Valery observed.

"Yes, but there was a price. Every week, every month, someone shows up at the Club and takes all our cash. Like that." Rupert snapped his fingers. "Without warning." He made a face and looked at Valery. "Now, with Carlos dead, I'll be able to own the Club all by myself. Assuming Mr Big agrees."

They both stared out the window for a while, and then Valery turned and went across the room to the desk where he kept his laptop. He sat down and opened the computer. Rupert looked over at him and muttered to himself. "That's all he ever does, the prick. Works at the computer. He spends his whole fucking time on the computer." He couldn't wait until he had seen the last of Valery. His instructions were clear, though. Valery was special, Valery was to be fed, Valery was not to be allowed out of the building.

"How long will we be stuck here?" he asked himself out loud. Todd was the one who would decide. Todd paid the money; Todd called the shots. Rupert wasn't sure, but he knew that Todd was pretty close to Mr Big, and suspected that in what they were up to now, Todd was simply acting as an intermediary, and that the money was really coming from Mr Big. Sooner or later, for a reason that Rupert neither knew nor intended to ask, he and Todd were to take Valery some place up north and let him work his computer magic there.

The money was good. Rupert had been promised half a million if it all went well. He had already received a good down payment. However, things weren't turning out quite as he had expected. Carlos had screwed things up at the very last moment by not agreeing to cooperate. Now, the whole thing had become very dangerous. Murder. No joke, that. Rupert hoped that Todd would get them to move fast, so that they would be out of the country before the police were on their trail.

"Where's Gloria?" The old tension was returning to him. There were times when he needed her, when he couldn't wait to take her by the waist, undress her, feel her, kiss her, and have her in their own special way. That was how he felt right now. He went to get another beer.

There was a noise at the door. Rupert and Valery both jumped to their feet. Rupert knew by the sound that it was Gloria. She slipped quickly into the apartment and closed the door behind her. "Hello," she said in a flat, exhausted voice.

"What's taken you so long?" Rupert asked. "Where have you been? What happened?"

"It went OK," she answered, looking around. "It stinks in here. You should open a window."

He grabbed her by the shoulders and shook her violently. "What happened?" I asked. "Tell me what happened."

She screamed. "Let go of me. Don't touch me." Rupert held her all the more tightly. "He shot him. Three times. He's dead. Is that enough? Will you stop it?" She struggled, attempting to strike Rupert in the face, and screamed again. "Take your hands off me. I need to pee. Badly."

"Where's Rolf? Is he with you?"

"No. He wants to stay on his own, for now."

Rupert looked at her with surprise. "On his own? Where?"

"Somewhere not very far from here."

"Does Todd know?"

"Yes."

Rupert shrugged and loosened his grip. "Where have you been?"

"Some hotel on the other side of the city. Not a nice place. A real dump. Now, will you let me go?"

Gloria went into the bathroom, locked the door, and started to undress in front of a big mirror. She was exhausted, she was emotionally drained, she was pissed off, she wished she could just disappear, she hated Rupert, she hated Todd, she hated them all. Her left eye still had a big bruise under it, and she tried not to look at it. As she slowly removed her clothes, one piece after another, her anger increased. She finally stood there naked, ready for her shower, ready to cleanse herself, examining herself critically in the mirror.

8

"May I come in?" Carmel asked.

The man in the large black leather chair sighed audibly from behind his desk. "Yes," he finally said. "Please do."

His office was more like a living room in Westmount than an office in downtown Montreal. His desk was in mahogany, with a red leather top. The floor was covered by a worn oriental carpet, and on the walls were paintings of horses pulling heavy wagons through the snow. Carmel guessed that Beaky Bechstein was a bachelor, and that he spent most of his life at the offices of John Bechstein and Associates, in the comfort of this room.

She offered to show him her ID, but he waved it to one side. "Please, have a seat," he said, pointing to a chair across the desk from where he sat.

Beaky was a tall, angular man in his sixties. His hands were veined and wrinkled by too much sunshine. He was clean shaven, had steely blue eyes, and a short fringe of grey hair around the back of his head. Above all, his nose was big and craggy. He was dressed simply—a beige shirt with long sleeves, beige trousers, and loafers of brown suede.

"Mr Bechstein," Carmel started, as she took her seat, "I would like to ask you a few questions concerning one of your colleagues, Richard Seaton." Beaky nodded impatiently, and she continued.

"At about five in the afternoon two days ago, his half-brother Carlos Antana was found dead in an apartment building here in Montreal. He had apparently been murdered. It was Richard who first discovered the body, and who called us. Since then, Richard has been helping us with our enquiries."

Beaky's face was dour. For some reason, it made Carmel think of curdled milk. It certainly sought to hide whatever was going on behind it. She could imagine that he was a bridge player in his spare time. Finally, he opened his mouth, part way. "I know," he said.

"Richard spoke to you?"

"Yes."

"Did he come into the office?"

"No. He called me from home."

"And what was your reaction?"

"My reaction?" He sounded surprised and said nothing, as though his reaction was self-evident, or possibly irrelevant. Carmel could feel those steely blue eyes settling calmly onto hers.

She tried again. "What did he tell you?"

"Just as you said. That his half-brother had been found dead somewhere here in Montreal, and that he was helping the police with their enquiries."

She struggled to contain her exasperation. "And what did you say?"

"I told him to stay away from work until the whole thing blew over." Beaky looked restless and impatient. He put a hand to his mouth and seemed to be reaching for his breath.

Carmel noticed this and decided that she would have to be careful not to upset him. "At present, we have no reason to suspect Richard of having done anything wrong."

"No. I'd be surprised if you had. Still, I think it's better for the firm that he stay away. At least for now."

"I need to learn about his movements over the last week. The times he spent here, at work."

Beaky nodded and spoke over an intercom. "Julia. Please join us for a moment." The girl who had greeted Carmel when she first arrived at the office came in and sat down. With the help of a little notebook, she confirmed what Richard had previously stated about Carlos' visit to the office on Tuesday, Gloria's phone call on Wednesday, and Gloria's second call followed by Richard's rapid departure on the Thursday afternoon of the murder.

When they were alone once more, Carmel asked Beaky if he thought that Richard was happy at his work. He rose and walked over to the window, where a vase of roses rested on a low table. He stooped to smell the flowers, and then turned back to face her, his tall profile outlined against the blue sky outside. "Yes. Very happy, I should think."

"Did he show any signs of stress or of burnout?"

Beaky waved the question away with the back of his hand. It seemed that nothing had been disturbing Richard recently.

"What sort of a person is he? How is he here at the office?"

"He's conscientious. Works well. Everyone here likes him. Is that what you mean?"

"Yes. Sort of."

Beaky felt compelled to continue. "He's rational. He acts deliberately. It wouldn't be his style at all to kill someone."

"What sort of work has he been doing?"

Beaky gave a deep sigh and scratched the side of his forehead. He returned to the big black leather chair and swivelled back and forth in it. "This is all very unfortunate," he finally said. "Really, it is."

There was a faded photograph of a woman in an antique silver frame that stood on the desk between them. Carmel thought that it must be a portrait of Beaky's mother, as the woman had a large nose, like his. It seemed to run in the family. "She must have been a bit of a matron," she said to herself. Like her Tante Agnes, who never married.

Beaky shifted the frame carefully an inch or two to one side, so as to have a clearer view of Carmel. "Can I assume that we will keep matters confidential? I don't want this thing, whatever it is, to become public. My firm is highly regarded, it has a first-rate reputation. You understand what I mean?"

Carmel nodded.

"You asked what sort of work Richard has been doing," he finally began. "Well. He has been doing a lot of defence work, largely for the Government of Canada. Mostly, in radar and communications systems."

Carmel leaned back and listened carefully. This could be interesting. Unfortunately, Beaky's voice trailed off into yet one more of his silences, so that after a while, she felt obliged to prompt him. "He told us that he had been specially vetted by the RCMP for that sort of thing."

"That is so."

"I imagine that you are anxious for Richard to be cleared rapidly of the murder so that he can get on with his work."

"Yes. And so that the Government not interrupt our contracts." He hesitated. "Yes," he said with a sort of long sigh. He seemed to be reaching a decision of some sort.

"Yes," he sighed again. "So that the contracts are not interrupted..."

"Do you think that's likely?"

"No. But if it did happen, well..." His voice trailed off.

Finally, he looked up at Carmel. "Ms Roch. There was something that happened this week. Something strange. There could be a connection, I just don't know. I think I must tell you."

"What was it?"

Beaky thoughtfully ran his tongue over his lips and took a deep breath.

"On Tuesday, last Tuesday, at the very end of the afternoon, I had a visitor. Unannounced. Like that." He flipped a hand in the air. "He never gave his name."

"Please describe him for me."

"About fifty years old, medium height, well spoken. A bland sort of face. He was wearing a light grey suit."

"Todd?" Carmel wondered to herself, her mind turning over rapidly. "Glasses? Did he wear glasses?"

"Not that I can remember..." Beaky stopped.

"You're sure?"

He reflected. "That's not so! I'm wrong. Yes! Of course, he was wearing glasses. At the beginning, he took them off and started to polish them with his handkerchief. It was a green silk handkerchief with an oriental pattern. Now I remember." He looked questioningly at Carmel. Could it be that she knew this man? he seemed to wonder.

"Describe their frame. Was it a black one? Or a brown one?"

"Of the glasses?" He thought for a moment. "No. Neither. They had a metal frame and metal rims."

Carmel nodded. "You say he didn't give his name. It wouldn't have been Todd?"

"Not that I know of."

"What happened next?"

"He said he had heard of the firm's expertise in systems engineering. Something like that. He then said that he represented a consortium of investors who might be interested in employing our services."

"How did you respond?"

"I was wary. There are consortiums and consortiums, after all."

"And so?"

"I asked if someone had recommended us. He didn't answer directly, but said that several persons had recommended us, and had spoken highly of one of our engineers. He was referring to Richard Seaton. He asked if Richard could take a special assignment."

Carmel felt the excitement rising within her. "What did he want Richard to do?"

Beaky held a hand up to restrain her. "I think I must have explained that we don't work like that. Clients deal with the Firm; their contact is with the Firm. They aren't given separate access to a specific engineer."

"His reaction?"

"He said that his clients would wish to have Richard provide the services, and no one else. He added that they would pay well, very well. For only a week's work, no more. In cash."

"In cash!"

"That is what he said."

"A week's work doing what?"

"I asked him the same question, but he refused to answer."

"What do you think?"

"Ms Roch. You're asking me to guess, and I wouldn't want to mislead you. All I can say is that what Richard has been working on recently relates mostly to the military radar sites that Canada and the United States operate jointly up in the north of Canada, and particularly in Labrador. He has been doing updates for some of their communications systems."

"I see."

"As you might expect, I became very angry. The man was talking like a crook and treating me like one, too. I asked him to leave. Also, I wasn't feeling well. I have a bit of a heart, you know, and it was beginning to act up."

Carmel smiled sympathetically.

"Just as he left, he said they would pay a lot of money, no questions asked. Under the table."

"Did he say how much?"

Beaky frowned in thought. "Something like a quarter of a million dollars up front, and another quarter of a million when it was done. Something of the sort. To be split between Richard, the engineering firm, and me. As I chose."

"Your reply?"

"I told him to get out, and said that if he returned, I'd call the police."

9

"So you see, Sonny, there may be a connection between the murder and Richard's work on the radar sites in Labrador." Carmel's voice revealed her excitement. "That's also where Emma comes from." It was Monday morning, and she had been eagerly waiting for him to get to the office so that she could tell him about her meeting with Beaky.

"Yes," he said thoughtfully, leaning back in the chair behind his desk. "Richard seems to be some sort of a focal point, but I still can't make any sense of it."

Carmel explained her thinking. "Todd visited Beaky on Tuesday, requesting Richard's services. He was turned down. He was then introduced to Richard by Carlos on Thursday, shortly before the murder. Perhaps someone murdered Carlos to block what Todd was trying to do. Perhaps Carlos was murdered because he failed to cooperate with Todd or threatened to blow the whistle on him."

Sonny shrugged. "I suppose. There are several possible explanations, but none of them make much sense to me. At least, not yet. At this point, we just have to keep our minds open."

She looked at her watch. "Meanwhile, there's a Mr Alfred Hamel who called this morning. He's the construction foreman down at the building where Carlos was murdered. Says he may have found something. I'm going down there to see him now."

"Good luck! And take your time, Carmel. If you push things too fast, you may overlook something that you know already." Sonny reached for a slim file in front of him and sighed. "In twenty minutes, I have to speak to the press and say a few things about a shooting that happened in Rosemont over the weekend."

She left Sonny thumbing through his file, and went to her own office, which she was sharing for the moment with Charles Gagné, stopping along the way to pick up a large cup of black coffee at the machine in the hall. The coffee was hot and burnt her tongue at the first sip. Gagné looked up as she entered the room. "Tell me, Charles, ever been to Labrador?"

"Can't say I have. Why?"

She said nothing, but started entering something on her computer.

LABRADOR, she read. POPULATION, ABOUT 27,000. My God, she thought. That wasn't very much at all. Less than half as big as Saint-Hyacinthe! She continued to read the website. 6,000 TO 10,000 BLACK BEARS. Ouf! Or rather, Grrrr. TOTAL AREA—OVER 100,000 SQUARE MILES. Impressive. Sounded bigger even than Florida. She checked. Much bigger! PRINCIPAL CITY: HAPPY VALLEY -GOOSE BAY, POPULATION 8,000.

She closed her computer and turned to Gagné. "Charles. I want you to join me for an hour or so. I have to go down to the condo where Carlos Antana was murdered. The construction foreman there has something he wants to show me." She finished her coffee and they left the office together.

"How was your weekend?" she asked, as he drove them down towards the Lachine canal in his Dodge Charger.

"Fine," he answered. "My wife's sister was visiting. What about you?"

"Great! I helped my brother bale some barley straw down at his farm."

"Where is it?"

"Near Saint-Hyacinthe."

"Oh! That's good land, down there," Charles said approvingly. "Is that where you were brought up?"

"Yes. It's the old family farm. Dairy. Very beautiful."

"How come you became a policeman, then?" It was something that Charles had often wondered.

"I went into the army when I was twenty. It was something I had always wanted to do. I stayed for eight years. When I got my release, it took me a while to find my feet. Someone suggested I try the Montreal police, and it seemed like a good idea. They really wanted to have me, because of my army experience, so I signed up. That was almost eleven years ago."

They soon reached their destination and headed down a ramp into the garage of the building, a large concrete cavern that smelled of fresh paint. Two men were quietly talking together at the side of an open container next to the door leading from the elevator. One was short and stout and wearing a blue wind jacket. The other was tall and thin and dressed in overalls that were spattered with white paint.

Carmel got out of the car and went up to them. "Mr Hamel?" she asked of the shorter of the two.

"Hello," he said, hitching up his trousers and putting out a plump hand. "Alfred Hamel." He spoke in the manner of the people from Beauce, southwest of Quebec City, and had difficulty with his aitches.

"I'm Carmel Roch, and this is Charles Gagné." She

looked around. "Do you come here every day?" she asked Hamel.

"Every day," he confirmed. "I'm the onsite supervisor."

"Could you tell me if the elevator was working last Thursday?"

"Yes, but not from the ground floor. We were pouring cement there, near the doors, and had to close off the area."

"And from the garage?"

"It was working normally. Anyone wanting to take the elevator upstairs from the garage, or to return from upstairs to the garage, could have done so."

Carmel nodded. "Tell me. Do you remember anything of the people who were occupying the top floor condo?"

Hamel thought for a moment. "Yes. I remember the older man, the one who was murdered. He seemed very friendly and liked to wave his hands around a lot as he talked."

"What about the others?"

"There was a tall guy. I didn't see much of him."

"Anyone else?"

"Yes. There was a woman. She was the one I saw most often. Quite something! Long red hair. Like a movie star." He rubbed his chubby hands together and rolled his eyes, which were round and beady.

"You saw her more frequently?"

"Yes. Down here in the garage, where she kept the cars."

"Cars?"

"She had a white Mercedes, a big one. She also had a little grey Toyota, a Prius. Sometimes she took the Mercedes, especially if the older man was with her. Often, though, she was alone, and just took the Prius."

"That's worth knowing. Now, please tell me what it is

that you have to show us.”

“I’m sure it’s nothing,” Hamel started, “but I felt that I should give you a call, just in case.”

“You never know,” Carmel said. “What is it?”

“A tarp, or maybe a bag, I’m not sure. One of the guys saw it in there.” He pointed to the container nearby. “We use it for construction rubble, leftover bits of plywood and plasterboard, that sort of thing. But this thing, whatever it is—none of us can remember having put it there.”

“When did you first notice it?”

“Last Friday. Sometime in the morning.”

Carmel walked around and took a few pictures, before standing on the tips of her toes and peering into the container. It was half full. All she could see was a tangle of scraps of plaster board, metal stripping and wrapping materials. “Where, exactly?” she asked Hamel.

He was up on a short ladder and peering into the container as well. Carmel hoped he wouldn’t fall in. “Right beneath you. You see that black thing? Partly under the sheet of plywood.”

She pulled herself higher and looked along the near side of the container. When she saw it, her heart started to pound.

A body bag! It was crumpled up and empty, but clearly a body bag. Just like the army ones they had used in Afghanistan. She dropped back down and leaned against the side of the container for a moment, trying to shut out the memory of those terrible moments when they had to scavenge for human remains in the burnt-out wreckage of an armoured vehicle, and place them into a body bag. Just like the one in the container.

“Do you want me to get it?” the workman asked, looking at her with a puzzled expression on his face.

Carmel swallowed hard. “Yes. Go ahead.” She pointed

to the gloves that were stuffed into his pockets. "Put those on first and be careful not to handle it too much."

He jumped into the container and carefully pulled the bag free, passing it up to Carmel. She examined it briefly, making sure it was completely empty, and took it over to the police cruiser, where she placed it in the trunk. She remained there for a moment, in silence. "Get a hold of yourself, Carmy," she told herself. The others were waiting for her when she returned.

"Why?" she asked herself. "Why did the murderer want to leave with the body? And why didn't he?"

She thanked Hamel and went upstairs with Gagné to look around the lobby of the building. There was nothing there that caught her eye, so they took the elevator up to the condo. The mess had been cleaned up.

Carmel looked about her with distaste. There was nothing to suggest that a man had spent his last moments there, probably in great pain, feeling his life ebb away, losing all hope for himself. The very cleanliness of the place seemed to make a mockery of death, and even of life itself.

"Nice place," Charles said to her as they went back down in the elevator. "Good location, too."

"Yes, but would you want to live here?"

He shook his head. "Not really. I prefer Ville d'Anjou. It's more like a village." The elevator reached the garage and they got out. "Why do you think they had two cars?"

She shrugged. "Perhaps Carlos liked the idea of being driven around in a flashy car, but Gloria wanted something smaller. That way, she could move around the city doing other things without being noticed. It's just a guess."

They took a last look at the container and got into Charles' cruiser. "Back to the station?" he asked her.

"No. Let's check something else first." She gave

Charles an address in lower Westmount. "Where Richard Seaton lives," she explained. When they arrived there, they had a quick look, and Carmel then asked Charles to drive along Sherbrooke Street to where Richard worked. Finally, from there, they drove down to the condo. "It all adds up—what he told us," she explained. "Now, we can go back to the station."

"You're amazing, Carmel," Charles said admiringly. "You're so organised. You never waste a moment."

She waved her hand dismissively. "I want to add something else to your list, Charles. Could you locate the rental business that provided the two cars? When you do, find out in whose name they were rented, dates rented and returned, mileages driven and so forth."

They reached the station, and Charles took the body bag off to the lab to see what they could make of it. Carmel went to see Sonny.

"So what was it?" he asked.

"A body bag."

He was intrigued. "A body bag! Assuming that the murderer threw it there, he must have brought it with him in the first place, intending to use it to take the body away."

"Carrying a body around isn't that easy," Carmel said. "It may mean that there was more than one person involved."

"Perhaps the murderer or murderers were surprised by Richard's arrival and had to get out of there fast before doing what they intended."

Carmel shrugged her shoulders. "In any event, the fact that it was in the container in the garage confirms that the murderer arrived and left by the garage."

"I guess you're right."

"The elevator wasn't working from the ground floor when it happened, but it was working from the garage.

So the murderer would have gone up and down from the garage in the elevator, while Richard went up from the lobby by the stairs."

"Uh-huh. So for example, the murderer arrived by the garage, went up with the bag in the elevator, shot Carlos, heard Richard arriving by the stairs, went quickly back down in the elevator, but without the corpse, threw the bag in the container, and left."

Carmel nodded. "Something like that."

"But why would he have wanted to leave with the body?" They both paused. That was the million-dollar question.

Carmel was the first to offer a possible explanation. "He may have intended to hide the body so that they would have a little extra time to do something else, the something else that they wanted to do up here in Canada."

"Possibly." Sonny had another idea. "Maybe they were going to leave in a chartered plane and take the body with them. You could ask Gagné to look up all the chartered flights that left Montreal last Thursday and Friday. Particularly the international flights."

He stopped to think for a short while. "I don't think he'll get very far, though. Why would they have gone to all that trouble just to take the body out of the country?"

Carmel sat there, her eyes closed, trying to understand why the man who murdered Carlos would have wished to leave the scene with the body. "We should ask Richard back for another talk," she said finally. "Perhaps we could learn something more from him."

"He called," Sonny said, looking slightly embarrassed.

"Good. I'd like to speak to him again."

"It won't be easy. He's not in Montreal. Said he needed a break. I couldn't tell him not to go. He's not under arrest, after all."

"Did he say where he'd gone?" She then remembered the bright eyes and the calm face framed in light brown curls that were tied back with a green ribbon. "Don't tell me. I think I know. He's gone to Labrador to see Emma."

"You're right. That's what he told me."

10

"Good morning, Carmy." Carmel was surprised that Charles was now taking the liberty of calling her by her nickname. It was alright with her, though. Good for morale.

"Hi Charles. How are they getting on with your office?"

"They were supposed to start painting the walls yesterday, but they never showed up. You're going to have to put up with me for a while longer. I hope you don't mind."

"No. Not all. Good to have a bit of company."

Carmel was putting some final touches on her notes from the day before, regarding Mr Hamel and the body bag, when she had a call from reception. She had a visitor, although she was expecting no-one. Intrigued, she went to see who it might be.

One glance sufficed—the red hair, the good looks, the bruised eye. Containing a mixture of curiosity and excitement, she put on a welcoming smile. "Gloria Marsham, I think."

Gloria was wearing a raw linen jacket with the cuffs

of the sleeves rolled back, an immaculate T-shirt, designer jeans, and no jewellery. She looked to be in her mid-thirties, perhaps a bit more. She was slim, and her golden red hair was carefully braided and tied up at the back of her head. Her neck was long, and her eyes were slightly slanted with high cheekbones. Her lips were straight, more thin than fleshy. She wore some makeup, including red lipstick and a thin layer of powder on the bruise under her left eye.

She stood looking carefully at Carmel, who had the sensation that she was being sized up. "Are you Ms Roch?" she asked. "Am I pronouncing your name correctly, please?"

Carmel nodded. "Yes, thanks. I'm Carmel Roch. Let's go in here where we can talk in private." She gestured towards the door of the small meeting room where she and Sonny had met Emma four days before. The two entered the room and Carmel shut the door behind them.

Gloria stood by a chair and looked at Carmel. "I came to see you about a small matter, small, but one that is very important at the same time." She spoke carefully, each word given its own space, and with more than a hint of a Slavic accent.

"You are most welcome. What is it that you wish to see me about?" For a moment, Carmel found herself speaking in the same clipped way as her visitor. It was ridiculous, but there it was.

"I understand that you are conducting the investigation into the murder of Mr Carlos Antana."

"Yes. I am."

"That is why I am here."

Gloria struck Carmel as being very sure of herself. She was certainly not the conventionally attractive, sexualised, brainless woman that Carmel had been given to expect. The two of them stood facing each other across the small table in the windowless room. You might have said two chess players, sizing each other up at the start of their game.

Carmel reached a hand up towards Gloria's left eye. "You hurt yourself," she said, looking as sympathetic as possible. "Poor you. That must have hurt."

Her visitor looked annoyed. "It's nothing. Just a bump. Stupid, really. I was carrying something, and I tripped." She looked around. "They don't give you very big meeting rooms."

"We have bigger ones for when there are more people."

"I see. However, a window would help."

Carmel smiled sweetly. "This way, it's more private." She then sat down. "You knew Mr Antana, I think."

Gloria settled into her chair. "Yes. I knew him well. I was his assistant. I helped him with many things." Her grey eyes glistened, and she reached into her sleeve for a small white handkerchief.

"We came here to Montreal about ten days ago," she continued, after dabbing at a teardrop that was slowly running down her cheek while Carmel watched in fascination. "He was a wonderful man, Ms Roch. Always kind. Always helping people. His death is a great loss for me."

Carmel murmured something to express her sympathy, and Gloria rapidly recovered her composure. "I am a married woman, Ms Roch. I am married to the man who was Carlos' business partner. Down in the Bahamas. But that doesn't mean that I was not close to Carlos as well. Carlos and me, we were like that!" She held up her hand emphatically, with two fingers neatly crossed. Carmel noticed that there was no ring.

Carmel couldn't help asking the question. "Where are you from, exactly? Do you mind if I ask?"

"Not at all. I am from a small town in Eastern Europe."

Gloria proceeded to name the small town, but so rapidly, and with such a strong accent that Carmel didn't stand a chance of understanding her.

A contained anger then came into Gloria's eyes. "I was born just after the end of the Soviet Union." She pronounced 'Soviet Union' with a peculiar snap, in a way that Carmel had never heard before. "It was not a good time, Ms Roch. Nothing but poverty. Poverty, violence, and dishonesty. I had no family." Her voice accelerated. "I got beaten. I got used. I won't tell you what I went through." She shook her head. "Terrible, it was. Just terrible."

Ukrainian, Carmel guessed. Infinitely smarter than she wished to appear. Come to see Carmel for no apparent reason. Not apparent just yet, in any case. "Tell me about Carlos," she said. "I know so little about his life after he left Montreal."

"After he left Montreal, Carlos went to Colombia. He told me all about it. He didn't know who his father was, but thought he might be Colombian. Something his mother had said, I think. So he went to Colombia to look for him."

"I see."

"He took various jobs, living down on the east coast in a town called Santa Marta. Not a big town. Apparently, a very small town. He was hoping to find his father, or at least to learn who he was. He was very unhappy that he didn't have a proper father." She threw her hands up in a wide gesture. "Why, I don't know. I never had one either. What's the difference, Ms Roch? What's the difference, as long as you're born with two arms and two legs?"

"And a head," thought Carmel, uncharitably.

"Finally, he went to the Bahamas."

"Is that where you met him?"

"Yes. But that came later. Carlos always loved the theatre. He was an actor. He liked to wave his hands in the air and use big words. Some of the words he used! He started a theatre, and my husband joined him. He was his business partner. They had a nightclub, and that went really well. It made a lot of money. They were a good team. Until now," she added, and her shoulders rose and fell in a suppressed sob.

"Was Carlos ever married?"

"No. But he was a kind man, Ms Roch. He gave money to charity. He sent money to schools for books, and to boys while they were studying. All over the world."

"And you?"

Gloria sniffed. "I used to go to the club, going with people, that sort of thing. You understand? I had to make a living, didn't I? It hasn't always been easy for me, Ms Roch. But then, I met my husband, and we were married. That was the start of a new life for me, and Carlos gave me a job doing various things."

"Your husband seemed to have a strong influence over Carlos," Carmel said.

Her visitor gave a warm smile and raised her hands in protest. "I don't know why you say that. My husband didn't push Carlos around. He doesn't push anyone around. He and Carlos were partners, that's all. It worked well." As Gloria continued to speak, she leaned forward, and the room, which was already small, seemed to become even smaller. Her voice became intimate, her perfume insistent. Carmel watched in awe as her hands, with their long delicate fingers, weaved patterns in the air.

"Tell me about your coming up here, to Montreal," Carmel asked.

"A fine city, Ms Roch. My first visit. Terrible what has happened. To Carlos, I mean."

"Yes. It was."

"My husband and I came with Carlos. We rented a

place to stay, an apartment down by the canal, and put on a show that Carlos had thought up, in a hockey rink. Carlos had a brother up here called Richard and was very anxious to see him again. Richard came to see Carlos at the apartment one afternoon and stayed for drinks and something to eat."

"Did they see each other apart from that? On another occasion?"

Gloria hesitated. "I think Carlos visited him at the office. He was so happy to see Richard again. It is extremely sad, what happened."

"Do you know anything about Richard, about the sort of work he has been doing?"

"No. I don't know Richard at all. I would hardly know him if I met him on the street. Carlos said he was very nice. He liked him."

"What about the day Carlos was murdered? Did he and Richard see each other again?"

For a moment, Gloria hesitated. Finally, she nodded. "Yes. Of course. In the car."

"Were you there?"

"Yes. I was driving."

"Anyone else in the car?"

She thought for a moment. "A friend of Carlos. Not someone I knew."

"Does the name Todd mean anything to you?"

Gloria shook her head. "No."

"Where are you and your husband staying now?"

"Somewhere just outside Montreal. Not a nice place. We will leave very soon. Almost at once."

"To go where?"

"Home. To the Bahamas, where we live."

"Who do you think may have wished to murder Carlos?"

"I don't know. I didn't kill him. I had nothing to do with it. You tell me. It's your investigation. Have you found anything?" She looked at Carmel expectantly.

"We have learned a thing or two," Carmel replied cautiously. "We know that you called Richard shortly before the murder, to warn him that something might happen. What was it that you were worried about?"

Gloria was quick to answer. "There was all that money lying around. Workmen in the building. You can't trust workmen. With money, you never trust anyone. Not if you're smart. I was worried for Carlos. Yes, I was worried for him." She fiddled with her sleeve and pulled out the handkerchief. She then thought the better of it and stuffed it back in again. "Do you think a workman might have done it?"

"Frankly, no."

"Are there other suspects, then? Do you have any suspicions?"

Carmel ignored the question. "Tell me, Mrs Marsham. Where were you at the time you called Richard?"

"I was waiting for a bus, somewhere in the north of the city." Gloria gave Carmel a smug look. "Did Richard go?" she asked. "Was it he who found the body?"

"Tell me, Mrs Marsham. Why exactly did you wish to see me?"

Gloria looked indignant. "What do you mean? I wanted to tell you what I know. Why not? Is there something wrong with that?"

Carmel was beginning to tire of the charade. "Nothing at all. It's just that you haven't told me very much."

Gloria went red in the face and she gradually exploded. "I came here to help you, and that's all you can say! What do you think I am, an animal? I don't want to be treated like an animal. Is that how you treat people here, in Canada?" She snatched up her handbag. "I'm going. I'm leaving. Right now. Goodbye!" They both got up, and Gloria was the first to reach the door.

"What was that all about?" Carmel asked herself with a laugh once her visitor had left. She immediately called Jean Perras and asked him to follow Gloria, to see where she would go.

Sonny was tied up, but when he became free, she dropped into his office in order to tell him about the meeting. "So you've met the lovely Gloria," he said. "Tell me about her."

Carmel grinned. "She's good looking, no doubt about that. And very smart. At the end, she faked getting angry so she could get out of here quickly. By then, she had achieved what she had set out to achieve, whatever that was. I had Perras shadow her after she left."

Sonny chuckled and tugged on his moustache. "What do you think she was after?"

"Her reason for coming? Perhaps to protest her innocence. I say that, but I'm not at all convinced. Certainly, to see where we have reached in our investigation. I think she may also have had some particular reason for taking the risk of coming, but I can't think of it just now. At least we now know that they're still in town."

"And did Perras find out where she went?"

"I wonder. Let's see if he's back." She dialled Perras and asked him to join them.

He appeared at the door a moment later, looking embarrassed. "I'm sorry, Carmel."

"Why? What happened?"

"I followed her into the Metro. She crashed the gate and took the train to Montmorency. I managed to get into the next car. She got out of the train at Jarry and caught a train in the other direction."

"And were you able to follow?"

"Yes. It was close, but I managed. But then she got out again at Jean-Talon. I did as well, but somewhere in the station she disappeared on me. I looked all over the place, but she was gone. I just got back a moment ago."

Carmel and Sonny smiled at each other. "Couldn't you see her hair?" Sonny asked. "That must have made it easier."

"No. She was wearing a beret. A brown one."

At this point, Carmel started to laugh. "When she left the office, she was wearing a white one. Don't feel bad, Jean. She's a real pro, that one."

Perras left, looking confused.

Sonny reached for a file on the console behind him. "Here are one or two things that the police in Nassau have sent to me concerning Carlos." He handed the file to her. "Nothing very exciting but have a look."

11

Carmel sat down at her desk and looked at the thin file in front of her. The yellow sticker on it read *Carlos Antana -Nassau Police*. She opened it.

There wasn't a lot in there. Carlos Antana was a respected citizen of the Bahamas. He lived alone in an apartment in central Nassau, owned a large building nearby where he ran a theatre and nightclub, and he had never been on the wrong side of the law, at least not as far as the Bahamian police were concerned.

He was active in a number of charitable works, and spent a lot of time and effort in sponsoring foster children, both in the Bahamas and abroad. A copy of a recent medical report attached to the file showed him to be in reasonable health. That was all. Nothing was said of Rupert and Gloria Marsham. Nor was there any mention of a man named Todd. The file also contained Antana's photograph, and Carmel examined it with curiosity. It was not a recent likeness, and it was also slightly blurred, but she thought she could recognise the round face and the curly blonde hair. The image seemed that of a happy man, full of self-confidence, at ease with himself. She got the impression that he must have been a nice person, harmless perhaps, but nice. Why would anyone have wanted to kill him?

The image of his body came back to her, lying there in the hallway in a pool of blood. What a sordid way for a man's life to end!

The idea came to her, suddenly, like an electric shock. She reopened the file that Sonny had given her and looked for the medical report. Antana's blood type was shown. It was A-positive, one of the most common blood types. No surprise there. She called Charles Gagné, who was not at his desk. "Hi Charles. Where are you?"

"I'm in Montreal West, looking for the Prius."

"I see. Have we received the pathologist's report yet?"

"Yes, in draft form. It's on my desk somewhere. Have a look, if you want."

"Thanks." She got up and went over to his desk. There were several folders lying under a green rock that Charles must have picked up on a hike somewhere. She found the draft report and took it back to her desk. "This is just routine, Carmy," she said to herself. "Don't get excited."

All the same, she felt a mounting fear that she might have made an enormous mistake. She thumbed rapidly through the document, looking for an indication of the dead man's blood type. Of course, it would be A-positive, the same as in the medical report that they had received from the Bahamian police.

She was wrong! It said O-negative. "Oh shit," she said. "This can't be." She read it twice, flipping back and forth between the two documents.

"They're not the same! Antana is A-positive, and the dead man is O-negative."

She jumped to her feet. "Jesus!" she swore. "We've screwed up completely. Sonny will be furious."

Sonny was tipped back in his chair with his shoes on the desk, reading a gardening catalogue. He put it down when she appeared and gave her an apologetic look. "What's up?"

She said nothing, but threw the two files down on his desk. She then pulled out the two documents, and laid them in front of him, open at the right pages. "Have a look!"

Sonny picked up the first one, the medical report for Carlos Antana. He then looked at the pathologist's report, and his eyes travelled back and forth from one document to the other. Frowning, he turned back to the cover pages of both, to make sure of what he was looking at. "Carmel. What are you telling me? Are you saying..." He held up the two documents. "They're not showing the same blood type! Is that it?" He looked at her.

She shook her head gloomily. "They're not the same man!"

He sat bolt upright and took another look. "The murdered man was not Carlos Antana! This is ridiculous. We've been completely wrong, all along."

"All along," she agreed.

"How could we have made a mistake like that?"

She produced two photos from the files and placed them in front of him. "Because they look so much alike. Here is the picture of Carlos Antana that we received from Nassau. And this," she added, showing him the second one, "this is the dead man."

"They do look alike," he agreed with a grimace, holding the two photographs up for both to see. "Very similar, in any case."

She sat down in the chair in front of the desk. "I saw the body myself, Sonny. I was able to have a good look at his face. When I saw the picture of Carlos in the file that you gave me, I found that it looked like the dead man. It never occurred to me that they might not be the same person."

"Didn't Richard identify the corpse last Friday?"

"Yes, he did. At the morgue."

Sonny's face flushed with anger. "The bastard. He misled us."

"I've been thinking of that. Of course, he may have done it on purpose. However, it could just have been an honest mistake. Before last week, they had barely seen each other since the brother was eighteen and Richard was twelve. Even over the last week, he only saw him two or three times. And corpses never look completely like the person did when he was alive."

"No. They don't."

"Sonny. That leaves us with an unidentified corpse, while Carlos Antana himself is out there somewhere, alive and kicking. Probably with the others. I bet Gloria has seen him. She must know that the murdered man wasn't Carlos Antana. In fact, now that I think of it, I think that the purpose of her visit was to find out if we knew. She's devious, that woman! I think she wants us to believe that Carlos is dead, when in fact he's not dead." Sonny was still examining the photos in front of him. He tugged hard on his moustache and looked up at her. "She may also know the identity of the murdered man."

"Probably." Carmel nodded her head. "Maybe she's the one who took him there in the first place. In the white Mercedes! Just so he could get murdered! By her or by someone else."

"The two men looking like each other. That's so strange."

"Sonny. We're going to have to think this whole thing through again, from start to finish."

"Yes," he mused. "And how!"

12

"How did you get on yesterday?"

Charles was waiting eagerly for her to sit down. "I found the taxi driver who took Richard down to the condo. His name is Prosper Dieudonné. He's Haitian."

"Good work. What did he have to say?"

"He confirmed everything. Time, place, even the rain shower. Everything."

"So Richard's alibi now seems complete. Anything else?"

"I found the rental company that owns the white Mercedes. It was returned last Thursday, by Gloria, at around twelve. They don't rent Toyotas, so I started checking the companies in Central Montreal with Toyotas. One had two leases that sounded promising. I spent the afternoon seeing what I could find out."

Carmel was impressed. "Go on."

"The first address was in Lachine. A grey Prius was parked outside, so I waited nearby, and watched. An old couple with suitcases came out of a side door and got in. I think they were tourists, up from the United States."

"Not them."

"No. The second address was in Montreal West. Same result. This time, the woman spoke French. By her accent, I think she must have come from New Brunswick."

"Not them either."

"No. But did you know that the big rental companies are getting a lot of competition these days from individual deals offered over the internet?"

"No, I didn't, but it comes as no surprise."

"Well, they are. I searched the Net and found a grey Prius that was offered for hire about two weeks ago by a guy who lives in Ville LaSalle."

"Did you check it out?"

"I contacted the owner of the car. He told me that the car was taken by a woman who just possibly has red hair, he wasn't sure, and that the car is due back tomorrow or the day after. The address the woman gave is on Saint-Denis Street. I was going to go there this morning."

"I'll go with you. Good to get out of the office for a change."

Montreal was looking wonderful, Carmel thought, as Charles drove them through the centre of the city on their way to Saint-Denis Street. It was a brilliant morning, with not a cloud in the sky, and the air smelled fresh and clear. Autumn was on its way.

There had been a lot of new construction, tall buildings for the greater part, and many of them of excellent design. She admired with pleasure the monumental entrance of the new university hospital and could see a steady flow of medical staff and patients passing through its doors. Further on, her eyes caught a gleam of light reflected off two thin glass towers that reached to the sky like silver stilettos, joining halfway up with a covered walkway. They made her think of two lovers holding hands.

She told Charles of her discovery that the murdered man wasn't Carlos, and of her meeting with Gloria. He was flattered to be taken into her confidence and asked a number of questions.

They reached Saint-Denis and Sherbrooke and pulled up outside a medium-sized apartment building, perhaps fifty years old, with a ramp leading to a parking garage below. "Let's go on down," Carmel said.

The garage was full of cars of all shapes and sizes, but there was no grey Prius to be seen. They parked the cruiser and went over to a door leading to the elevator. A young woman was coming out when they arrived, and held the door open for them. "Excuse me," Carmel said to her. "Does the building have a superintendent or janitor?"

"Yes," she replied. "Janos. Are you looking for him?" She didn't wait for an answer. "Apartment 201. He's an older man, and lives alone."

Carmel thanked her and she and Charles went up to the lobby. They rang the bell of apartment 201 several times, but there was no reply. Nor was Janos anywhere to be seen.

"Let's try his door," Charles suggested. They went up a floor, and after knocking on the door of apartment 201, concluded that Janos wasn't there either.

On their way back to the lobby, they shared the elevator with a young man carrying a packsack full of books, obviously a student on his way to classes. He hadn't seen Janos either. Carmel asked him if there were any short-term rentals in the building. He said he thought that there were. She went on to describe Rupert and Gloria to him, and showed him the photo of Carlos as well, and asked if he had seen anyone answering their description.

The student thought for a moment. "No. But perhaps you should try the top floor. There's an apartment there that sometimes gets rented out. The owners are Chinese. There were people there recently, I think. It's on the front of the building," he added.

They thanked him and took the elevator up to the top floor. At the front of the building was a single door, and they knocked. There was no reply. They knocked again, several times.

Carmel made a face. "I think there's someone in there," she said to Charles. They took turns putting their ears close to the door, and finally, Charles nodded.

"I can hear something," he agreed.

The noise was barely audible and was coming from low down, just inside the door. It was a scratching or a rasping noise and seemed to be coming from under the door itself. "Hello," said Carmel, thumping her fist on the door. "Is anyone there?" There was no answer, but the noise stopped, and then started again, more insistently.

"I heard a moan," Charles said. "I'm sure of it."

Carmel stood back from the door. "Open up. It's the police," she said in a loud voice.

There was no reply, and she aimed a ferocious kick at the lock of the door. The lock sprung immediately and the door swung open part way. They could see that there was something inside on the floor that was blocking it.

Carmel stepped through the partly open door, and Charles followed her. Turning back towards the door, they saw a body lying across a small carpet. Carmel immediately knelt beside it, while Charles went off to check the rest of the apartment. "Is he alive?" he asked when he returned. He looked with horror at the body on the carpet. "What happened to him? Shall I call an ambulance?"

"Yes, right away." Carmel felt so sorry for the man lying in front of her that she could scarcely talk. "Also, bring some water."

He was an older man and had been savagely attacked. His breathing was irregular, and he seemed only semi-conscious. His mouth was clamped shut and smeared with dried blood, and a front tooth dangled outside his lower lip by a thread of flesh. Around one eye, the face was so swollen that the eye itself was barely visible. One arm lay towards the door, the hand resting on the woodwork. The other arm was held tightly to his stomach, as if to contain the pain that he must have felt there as well. Carmel looked carefully beneath his hand, and could see that there was also damage there, possibly broken ribs.

Charles arrived with a glass of water, and she put it to the man's lips. At first, the water simply flowed down onto his chest, but finally, his mouth opened slightly, and his throat made a swallowing motion. "Janos?" Carmel asked softly. There was no immediate answer. "Janos," she whispered in his ear, bringing the glass of water once more to his lips, "Janos. You're going to be fine. Hang in there. Everything is going to be alright."

She asked Charles to bring a damp towel and used it to wipe the man's forehead. He had a brush cut of grey hair, and she passed the towel over it as well. A moment later, they heard an ambulance arrive in the street below, and Charles went out to meet it. Within ten minutes, Janos was on his way to the hospital nearby.

An elderly woman in a purple dressing gown had been standing to one side in the hallway, watching what was going on. "This is terrible!" she exclaimed, when Carmel went up to her. "Wasn't that Janos? On the stretcher?"

"I believe so," Carmel answered. "Do you live in the other apartment?" She nodded towards a door at the other end of the hallway.

"Yes. Down there."

Carmel identified herself and asked if the woman

had heard or seen anything that could reveal what had happened to Janos.

"Yesterday at around six in the afternoon, I heard some loud voices. I thought the noise came from outside. Finally, I looked out into the corridor, and saw that the people who had been living here for the last week were leaving. One was carrying a large aluminium suitcase. The woman had a small bag."

"How many were they?"

"Three. A tall man with dark hair. A small man with curly hair. And the woman."

"What was the colour of the woman's hair?"

"I couldn't see. She was wearing a beret. A younger woman, I would say. And quite pretty. She seemed to be the one in charge."

"Can you tell me anything more about their appearance? Please make an effort. It's very important."

The woman reflected. "The short man limped. That's about all I can remember."

"You say that they had been living here for the last week. Had you seen much of them previously?"

"Very little. I don't go out very often. I saw the taller man once, perhaps. Not the other two. They had a car."

"How do you know?"

"One of them mentioned it. As they were leaving, he asked the woman with the beret if she had the car keys. She checked in her handbag and then said 'yes'." The woman hesitated. "Actually, what he asked was 'Do you have the keys to the Prius?' Comes to the same thing, I suppose."

Carmel thanked the woman, and Charles took a note of her name and telephone number. They returned grim-faced to their car in the garage. "That poor guy," Charles said. "He must have seen something, or said something."

Carmel nodded. "Nasty, Charles. Really nasty.

Whoever it was, hit him again and again, in the face and on the body. It was senseless and vicious. Only a psychopath would act like that."

Charles blanched. "Where do you think they've gone?"

"Charles. I'll tell you what I think. I think that Todd, Gloria and Rupert, and now, it seems, the man with the limp and the curly hair, are here in Canada to do something illegal that is connected with our radar sites. The military ones, up north. Especially the ones in Labrador that Richard has been working on. I think that's where they've gone."

"To Labrador?"

"Yes, to Labrador. That's where Richard is right now."

"You think they've taken the Toyota?"

"Yes. There's a road, isn't there? Through Baie Comeau and Labrador City?"

"I think so. I'll put out a search for the Toyota, now that I know its license plate number, and I'll keep in touch with the owner, in case it shows up somewhere."

Back at the office, Carmel went to discuss the file with Sonny, and to tell him what had happened. He listened in silence, and finally leaned back in his chair, pulling softly on his moustache. "Carmel. If, as you say, we're dealing with a plot involving Canada's radar system, then we're going to have to get the RCMP involved."

She frowned. "I'll leave that to you. It sounds complicated."

"Complicated? A complete nightmare! In my experience, they can be impossible to deal with."

"Then let's wait a bit before we talk to them."

Sonny looked at her. "It's even worse. Those radar sites are jointly managed with the United States. The Mounties would want to get the Americans involved as well. In fact, they would have no choice."

They sat there in silence. "Sonny," Carmel finally said. "There's too much that we don't know. We need more facts. I think I should go to Labrador. I'd like to ask Richard a thing or two. In any event, Labrador seems to be coming into the equation more and more. What do you think?"

"Go ahead," he said slowly. "But for God's sake, be careful. These guys are dangerous."

"Sergeant Detective Carmel Roch of the Montreal Police," she announced, removing her dark glasses and showing him her ID.

He started to write her name down, but hesitated. "Spelled R O C H, but pronounced ROCK," she explained. Carmel was not in uniform, as she hadn't wished to attract attention. When she was in the field, investigating or looking for someone, she felt more comfortable in street clothes.

The police officer in front of her said nothing as he examined her ID. He was a big man, broad shouldered, in his forties, with a plain open face and reddish hair. He finally looked up and gave her a welcoming smile. "I'm Jim MacAbby of the RCMP. Welcome to Goose Bay. What brings you here?"

"I'm following up on a murder which occurred in Montreal about ten days ago. I only arrived today. It seemed right that I should come to say hello when I got here."

MacAbby thanked her. "You didn't really need to,

but I appreciate the gesture." He paused to wipe his brow. "Quite hot today," he explained. He glanced at Carmel. She was wearing a grey tracksuit with a hood and a green tuque. "If she finds it cold now," he seemed to be saying to himself, "she'd better not come here in January."

Carmel had only wished to pay a courtesy call on the RCMP, nothing more. She and MacAbby exchanged one or two generalities, and then she rose from her chair. "Nice to meet you," he said to her at the door. "Just let us know if there's anything we can help you with."

She put her dark glasses back on and stepped outside. Now that she had checked in with the Mounties, she intended to drive around Goose Bay in order to get a general idea of its layout. That wouldn't take too long. Then she would start with the hotels.

Her main purpose was to catch up with Richard, but she was also increasingly convinced that the others were on their way up to Labrador as well. That morning, she had telephoned Charles from the airport. He informed her that the Prius had shown up, abandoned in the street the night before outside its owner's home, with everything in order and the keys on the seat. Carmel had asked him if it had done a lot of mileage whilst in Gloria's possession.

"You'll never believe this, Carmy," he said. "Two thousand eight hundred kilometres in just under two weeks. I think that when they left that day, after they beat up the janitor, they made a long trip somewhere, a very long one."

Carmel thought for a moment and then agreed. She made a quick calculation. By driving about twelve hundred kilometres, Gloria could have taken the others from Montreal up to the start of the Trans-Labrador Highway, at Wabush or Labrador City. She could have left them there and returned to Montreal to get rid of the car.

After that, she could have gone back to join them, by plane or by bus. They could then have rented a new car, this time with Newfoundland and Labrador plates, and driven the five hundred kilometres or so down to Goose Bay. They might even have arrived by now.

Carmel got into her rented car and set out to explore Goose Bay. It was all very neat and tidy, but the town was spread out and lacked charm. She drove around for a while, but it didn't take long before she had seen all that there was to see.

She went to several hotels to ask if they had a Richard Seaton staying as a guest. None of them had. She booked herself a room in one of them. It was more like a motel than a hotel, and on two floors. Each room was a sort of suite, with a kitchenette and its own door leading directly to the outside. If you went up a flight of stairs on the outside of the building and walked down a long outdoors balcony, her room was in the middle.

By four o'clock, she was getting hungry, so she went for a bite to eat in a nearby restaurant. An Indian woman in a sari showed her to a table by the window. The only other customers were two older Inuit women who were watching a tennis match on a video screen on the wall.

The woman in the sari looked down at her, holding an order pad in her hand. "What can I get you, my dear?" Carmel took a quick look at the menu and ordered a club sandwich.

A few minutes later, an Indian man in his twenties appeared from outside. "Anand," the woman called to him. "Come here with me now." She went into the kitchen and emerged a moment later with a cardboard box containing a hot pizza, which she handed to him. "Take this now. Fourteen Campbell Street." Anand promptly disappeared to do her bidding.

While Carmel lingered at her table, this process was repeated several times, and it occurred to Carmel that if Richard, or for that matter any of the others, was holed up somewhere in Goose Bay and was anxious not to be seen, ordering takeout meals would be one solution.

That evening, just as she was having a beer at a bar near her hotel, her cellphone buzzed. There was a text message from Charles Gagné.

SORRY TO BOTHER YOU. CHECK YOUR EMAILS. CHARLES.

She downed the rest of her beer and returned to the hotel. Back in her room, she took out her laptop and found the email from Charles. "Hi Carmy. You'd better read the attached. Sonny got it from Interpol." She flicked over to the *pdf* that came with the email and started to read.

*"Genadi Todaglù. Age: approximately 50. Place of birth unknown. Lives mostly in Istanbul and Sofia. Speaks six or seven languages fluently. Carries several passports using a variety of identities and names, including Gentile, Nagilù and Todd."*

A photograph followed, and even if it was out of date and out of focus, Carmel could see that the face corresponded to what she already knew about Todd.

The extract went on to relate that during the second war in Iraq, Todaglù had been able to buy large quantities of mortar shells and small arms munitions and sell them in Iran. Later on, he helped Iran circumvent the embargo on its oil exports. Then he developed several sources for short-range missiles and military drones. He became quite close to the Russians and was thought to have helped them infiltrate spies into Israel and Egypt. Most recently, he had narrowly escaped arrest in the north of Norway, where he was attempting to get onto a radar site with a Russian agent in tow. Todaglù avoided publicity, kept a low profile, and was known to be ruthless and highly dangerous.

Carmel read and reread the *pdf* several times. It all seemed so familiar. In Afghanistan, people like Todaglù had been everywhere; the country was a perfect playground for turncoats and scoundrels. She had met more than her fair share of them in the councils and committee meetings of Kabul, and at a more local but equally lethal level, in Kandahar and the small villages scattered nearby, along the Arghandab.

She found herself bristling with anger, with hatred for such people, peddling weapons and munitions for gain, and poisoning the politics of failed and defenceless states.

14

The next morning, she called Sonny. "How's Janos?" she asked. She had been worrying about the superintendent of the building on Saint-Denis Street ever since she left Montreal.

"Fine. He'll be alright. Charles visited him at the hospital yesterday."

"What happened? Did Charles find out?"

"Yes. It seems that there were two men and a woman staying there, and that when he saw that they were about to leave, he went upstairs to say goodbye and made a comment about some empty beer cans that were lying about. The taller man, by his description it must have been Rupert, flew off his handle and punched him several times in the face, and when the poor man fell to the floor, he started kicking him. Broke two ribs."

"A psychopath, Sonny. That man Rupert's a psychopath."

"They're a bad bunch. Did you read the note about Todaglù, or whatever his name is?"

"Yes, I did. Another hard case."

"Do you have your pistol with you?"

"No. I left it in Montreal. On purpose." She heard Sonny give a grunt at the other end of the line.

"Speaking of pistols," he said, "the murder weapon may have been a Walther. In any case, the bullets were 22 caliber Long Rifle, coated lead with a hollow point."

"Small, but good enough at close range. And not too noisy."

"Yes," he agreed. "A woman's gun." Carmel winced, but he had a point. Sonny continued. "This thing about Todaglù really worries me. It seems to confirm what you have been saying all along, that the murder is part of something much bigger, something that involves a plot to break into one of our radar sites."

"That's what I think," Carmel confirmed.

"I'm going to have to speak to the RCMP in Ottawa, and maybe even to CSIS." She could hear him swear softly to himself. "What are your plans now?" he asked.

"I still have to find Richard. I'll look around here for a while longer, then I'll make a quick trip up the coast to where Emma lives, in Makkovik."

That afternoon, she decided to go down to the supermarket to buy one or two things. It was about three-thirty when she arrived, and she left her car in the parking lot just in front. She entered the store and went to the dry goods section to pick up some shampoo. She then crossed over to the food section to look for some fresh vegetables to eat in her room.

There was a man standing in the end row looking at dairy produce. He gave her a quick, curious look. He was short, and his head was bald and round as a melon. Carmel returned his glance, and he quietly turned away. Picking up his basket, he headed towards the checkout. Carmel found this odd. He hadn't selected any of the dairy goods he was looking at. He just drifted away, as though he had recognised her, and didn't want her to notice his presence.

She tried to think if she knew him, if she had ever seen anyone like him before, but could think of no-one. Acting on intuition, she followed the man over to the checkout and waited quietly behind him. Before she knew it, he had deposited his basket on the floor near the cash register and slipped out the door without stopping to buy anything.

Carmel arrived outside just in time to see a white Honda Civic pulling away. The strange man with the bald head was sitting in the passenger's seat, and Carmel could see a woman wearing a white beret hunched over the wheel. Women in Labrador wore tuques, not berets! It had to be Gloria.

Carmel raced over to her own car and left the parking lot just as the Honda was disappearing down the main street, heading east. She followed it, her hands gripping the wheel and her right foot hard on the accelerator.

The Honda was moving fast and turned left at the first intersection. Carmel followed suit with a flying turn and managed to close the gap between them. Her blood was up! However, the Honda did a last minute left up another road, and almost lost her as it accelerated away. Gloria sure knew how to drive a car!

Soon, Carmel was falling behind again. Her car was unfamiliar. It was certainly no equal to the cruisers she was used to driving with the Montreal Police. She stepped harder on the gas. Stop signs and street names flashed by: Churchill, Campbell, Learning, Lethbridge. They were crossing a quiet residential area, but the Honda didn't let up. Finally, it emerged onto the main road again, this time heading out towards the airport, and in a desperate attempt to follow, Carmel blasted through a red light and swerved at the last moment to avoid hitting a black pickup truck that skidded to a halt in front of her. Her tyres screamed, and the driver of the pickup leaned on his horn and shook a big fist in the air.

A moment later, she heard the wail of a police siren and saw the flashing red light of an RCMP cruiser coming up from behind. "Merde!" she swore as she pulled over to the side of the road. "Double merde!"

A constable emerged from the cruiser and came up beside her car. He motioned for her to roll down the window.

Carmel looked out and gave a sigh of relief. "Hello, Jim," she smiled sweetly. "It's me."

"Oh," said Jim MacAbby, as he scratched his head. "It's you!"

"I was following a car. A white Honda."

Jim just looked at her, and she realised that she was going to have to tell him a lot more than that. "Perhaps we should go down to the station and have a little talk," she said.

Twenty minutes later, they were sitting together in his office, and she was filling him in with details about Gloria, Todd and Rupert, and touching briefly on her suspicions as to why they had now come to Labrador.

Jim was particularly curious about Gloria's passenger and asked her for a description. "You know, Carmel. The RCMP has a lot of mugshots on its files. Do you want to see if you can recognise him?"

"Great idea," she said. "If the program lets you, filter it to white males."

He started up his computer, and she pulled her chair over to where she could have a look. Image after image came up on the screen. "We're now in the international section," he announced. He kept flashing up images. Suddenly, Carmel almost jumped out of her seat. "Stop! Scroll back." She took a careful look. "That's a possibility. That could be him! What's his name?"

Jim peered at the screen. "Valery something," he said. "I can't pronounce the last name. S H T I S K I N."

"What do they say about him?"

"He's Russian. A colonel in the army. Born in Saint Petersburg, 1982. Expert in defence systems and electronic warfare. Known to have worked in a…" Here, he spelled it out again. "… a S P E T S N A Z hacking network in 2016. Possibly involved in a recent abortive attempt to break into a radar site in northern Norway. What do you think?"

Carmel leaned forward and examined the image. "Jim. It sure looks like him, and there's this stuff about radar sites. It's got to be him. We've found our man!"

He turned off his computer, and she moved back to where she faced him across his desk. "I don't think we should broadcast the news in your force until we have a more positive identification. What do you think?"

He nodded thoughtfully. "I agree. We should be certain first. How, I don't really know, but still. What are you going to do next?"

"Keep looking around." She grinned as she rose to leave. "I'll do my best to stay out of trouble. In any event, I now owe you one. If you ever come to Montreal and get into trouble, you can count on me."

"If I ever go to Montreal…" he started.

"Yes. Is there something in particular you would like to do?"

Jim looked at the ceiling. "It's just that I would really love to visit the Olympic Stadium."

Carmel laughed. "Easy. I live just next door."

Back at the hotel, Carmel called Sonny. She started

off by telling him about the car chase. He was less than impressed. "Dumb, Carmel," he said. "Just plain dumb. Now, Gloria and the others know you're in Goose Bay, following their trail. You'll have set all the alarm bells ringing." She had to admit that he had a point.

"Hang on, Sonny. There's a plus side. Do you remember the description we had of the second man who was staying at the apartment on Saint-Denis Street? With Rupert? We were given it by the lady who lived next door. She said he was short, with curly hair, and he limped."

"Yes."

"Well, the man who got into the car with Gloria when I chased them all over Goose Bay was bald, and he didn't limp."

"Not the same man."

"Yes, but he was short. I think it was the same man. It's just that in Montreal, he wore a wig and faked the limp."

"Ah."

"Afterwards, I went back to the RCMP station to make my peace with the officer I know there, whose name is Jim MacAbby. He had the idea that we should see if I could recognise the man with the bald head from their file of mug shots. We spent some time together looking at faces, and finally I recognised our man. What do you think?"

"What?"

"He's a Russian spy!" She paused for effect.

There was a long *Whaaaaat* on the other end of the line.

"Sonny! Believe me. I'm not kidding. He's a colonel in the Russian army. His name is Valery Shtiskin, and he's an expert in electronic warfare and electronic defence systems."

Sonny grunted. "I hope you're not kidding me,

Carmel. If so, I'll never forgive you."

"Sonny. It's the truth, believe me."

"You've been chasing a Russian spy around Goose Bay, and he was in a car driven by Gloria."

"Correct."

"Absolutely sure?"

"Cross my heart and hope to die."

"Now, I'm certainly going to have to talk to the RCMP. We can't just shut up about that. I think I'll go to Ottawa in person. I have one or two good contacts there."

"That could help," Carmel agreed. "How do you think they'll react?"

"I hate to think. Spell his name for me, please."

She did so. "Sonny, in the extract from the file that Charles sent me on Todaglù, they say that he was almost caught trying to take a Russian spy on to a radar site in Norway. Do you remember that?"

"Yes, now you mention it. You think that spy was Valery Shtiskin?"

"Chances are."

"And who was murdered in Montreal, then? Who was he, and who murdered him?"

"And why? I don't know yet, but I think the answer's up here, in Labrador somewhere."

15

The Twin Otter droned northwards on its way to Makkovik, hitting every possible air pocket along the way. The plane was almost full and had an interesting assortment of passengers. Some were Innu, but most were Inuit, or men and women of mixed Inuit and European blood.

Carmel stared out the window at the country below, fascinated by the endless patchwork of bare rock, muskeg, and stunted black spruce. There were ponds and lakes, streams and rivers, all with meandering edges of vegetation that she supposed to be alder and willow. What particularly caught her eye were the areas of caribou moss and lichen, traversed mysteriously by what could only be animal paths, and spreading out in long splashes of creamy white with inexplicable blotches and whorls of russet and yellow. The landscape was changing, for sure. "I'm heading north," she thought, with anticipation and a touch of apprehension. "North, where Richard may be. North, where the radar sites are!"

The plane landed on a short runway lying in a broad valley of mosses and low vegetation, set amongst rolling hills. A small building and one or two bits of equipment stood at one end, but there was little else to see. The skies were blue, and the air had a fresh, salty tang to it. Carmel was able to hitch a lift into Makkovik from a fellow passenger, in a rusty black pickup truck.

They drove up a long slope of black spruce and caribou moss and came to a modern school building with what looked like an indoor sports facility beside it, perched on the crest of the hill. Gazing ahead to their left, Carmel could see the broad ocean, its sparkling surface stretching away to an indistinct horizon. The village itself lay at her feet, comfortably settled along the shore of a small inlet. Across the water on the further side was a long ridge of rock cliffs and caribou moss, crisscrossed with straggling lines of short shrubs and stunted black spruce trees.

A wide gravel road took them down to the water's edge. Some sixty houses and one or two community buildings were scattered about, and a pretty wooden church stood off to one side. Carmel got out beside a fish-packing plant that stood at the near end of a large wharf, thanked her driver, and had a look around. There was a pleasant smell of fish and seaweed in the air.

Out on the wharf, a man on a forklift was bringing a stack of wooden pallets back to take their place beside some empty containers. Closer by was a tangled pile of crab traps, leaning against the side of a pale blue metal shed. An old dinghy lay upended beside her, its wooden bottom bruised and peeling. Off to her right, Carmel could see a stretch of open water, with one or two small fishing dories riding at anchor.

She stood there bemused, feeling that the whole thing was faintly unreal. It was certainly unlike anywhere she had been before, and she had travelled a lot, more than most, it seemed to her.

When they first met in Afghanistan, she and Jean-Claude had taken that memorable trip together to Sri Lanka, where they had fallen deeply in love. Back at the Canadian base in Kandahar, they had been obliged to cool it, because he was a commissioned officer with a brilliant career ahead of him, and she was other ranks. However, more trips followed, to equally exotic places. Yes. She had travelled. But this place, this sleepy little out-of-the-way fishing port, was different, and it really charmed her.

She slung her bag across her shoulder and walked along a beach of rough stones to have a look at the boats that were moored out in the water. What immediately caught her attention was a white boat, seven or eight metres long, tied up along the near side of a small wooden jetty. The curve of its hull was graced by a long navy-blue line, and at the bow, she could read its name, *WALRUS*, painted black in a proud script. Above was a low cabin with two rectangular windows, and on its roof, a short mast for radar and communications. The cockpit had a windscreen and captain's chair, and behind that and below, there was a place for people to sit. The overall impression was of solidity and reliability.

As she arrived, a woman poked her head out of the cabin and looked at her. She was dressed in yellow waterproofs and black rubber boots, and her curly brown hair jutted out from under a black tuque. Carmel immediately saw that it was Emma. "Hello," Emma said. "Is there something you want?"

She paused and suddenly gasped. "It's you! The woman from the police." She was obviously taken aback by Carmel's sudden appearance. "Is everything alright?" She stepped off the boat and onto the wharf.

The two of them stood there for a moment, facing each other. Carmel wondered if Richard was there as well,

WALRUS

in the boat. The ridiculous thought occurred to her that Richard was actually quite tall, that he couldn't possibly fit into such a small boat. She found Emma's Labrador accent even stronger than what she remembered from their meeting in Montreal.

"Yes, it's me, Emma. Carmel Roch. And everything's alright. Please don't worry. I'm up here for a day or two, that's all. I was hoping to catch up with Richard and ask him one or two more questions."

Emma grasped Carmel's arm and looked into her face. "He's not in trouble, is he?"

"No. Not at all. Quite the contrary. His office has confirmed what he told us, and so has the taxi driver who drove him down to the condo. This means that he was almost certainly somewhere else when the murder was committed and has a strong alibi."

Emma's face cleared and she withdrew her hand. "Thank God!" she said. "Thank God for that. He's not here, though. He left yesterday. Why do you want to see him?"

"Richard was here. With you? Then he left?" Carmel laughed softly to herself and found herself thinking that she should have stayed in Goose Bay.

"Yes. He left on the afternoon plane."

"May I come onto your boat? Could we have a little talk?"

Emma nodded and reached out a hand to help her. "Should I call you Carmel?"

"Yes. Please do."

Emma gestured towards an opening that led below. "Want to look inside? I've fixed it up really nicely."

Carmel accepted and eased herself down the short ladder that led inside the cabin. She couldn't stand up properly, but had to stoop, and it was dark in there, so that it took a moment for her eyes to adjust.

At the bow, she could see a deep shelf that went from one side of the boat to the other. She guessed it was a bunk, as there were two navy blue sleeping bags, neatly folded, placed at its top. Closer to where she stood was a narrow table in mahogany, with a matching bench, and above it on the wall, various items of electronic gadgetry. To her left was a cooking area, two gas burners with a small fridge below, and on the near side, a short bookshelf with a variety of charts and manuals. Just behind her was a small door, which she supposed led to a toilet. All was very neat and tidy, and every inch of space was put to use.

She returned to the cockpit, and they sat down facing each other. Emma was far more relaxed than she had been when she came to see Carmel at the police station the morning after the murder. Carmel guessed that the boat was where she most liked to be. She could see its name printed on a life jacket: WALRUS. The boat was short and beamy, and the name suited it very well.

"What happened," Emma explained with a shy smile, "was that just before I came home, Richard and I had lunch together in Montreal. It was a really nice lunch, and he sort of invited himself to join me on my boat, when I was to bring it back up here."

"So he joined you for the trip? Did it take long?"

"Three days." Emma gave another little smile. "It was good. We got along really well together. He said it helped him get over his brother's death. But then, he had to return to Montreal to clear one or two things up. Once he's done, he's going to come back again."

For a moment, the two of them were distracted by the noise some seagulls were making nearby, fighting over a scrap of fish. "What was it that he wanted to clear up?" Carmel asked. "Do you mind telling me?"

"No. Not at all. Mostly, he wanted to talk to you."

Emma thought for a moment. "You see. When we got here, he wanted to use his laptop. He couldn't make it work. At first, he didn't take notice. He thought it was our Wi-Fi at the house. But it wasn't that, and he discovered that it wasn't his laptop at all. That's what he wanted to tell you."

She gave a little laugh. "He was really upset. All through our trip north, he had taken such care of it. The wet. The salt air. All of that. And then, he found out it wasn't even his!"

"Did he know what had happened? Did he say when he might have ended up with the wrong laptop?"

"Yes. He said it was in a car he took. People giving him a lift to the office."

That was Gloria, Carmel thought to herself, handing him the laptop he had forgotten in the car, with a big smile, on the Thursday morning of the murder. She had deliberately done a switch.

That meant that they had Richard's computer, which probably contained all sorts of information on the work he had been doing, and in particular, on the radar sites he was involved with. They couldn't hire him, or get at him in some other way, so they stole his laptop instead. But could they crack it, get through the passwords and encryption? Not Rupert or Gloria, she thought. Not even Todd. Perhaps that was a job for the Russian. Melon Head. Yes, she decided, he could well have an expertise that would permit him to get into Richard's laptop.

"Tell me, Emma. Did Richard ever mention the others to you? Todd? Rupert? Gloria?"

"No. Well, that's not quite true. We discussed Gloria a bit."

"What did he say?"

"That she seemed very friendly. Perhaps closer to Carlos than to the others."

"She is married to one of them. To Rupert."

"Not for real. At least, that's what Richard thinks."

Carmel nodded. "Have you seen anyone suspicious up here in Labrador since you returned?"

Emma gave her a worried look. "No. Nobody like that."

"Did Richard ever mention the work he has been doing up here on the radar sites? Did he ever mention any sites in particular?"

"Never."

Carmel still had to determine whether Richard truly believed the dead man to be his half-brother. The whole point of seeing him again was to learn whether he had made an honest error in identifying the body, or whether he had deliberately misled the police. For now, however, she didn't wish to tell Emma that Carlos was still alive. It was instinctive—you didn't reveal things like that unless there was a reason to do so. And she certainly wasn't going to tell her about Todaglù and Shtiskin.

"Has Richard been in touch with you since he left?" she asked Emma.

"No. He said he would call me from Montreal."

"From Montreal! So he flew from here to Goose Bay, and was going to take a connecting flight to Montreal."

"That's right."

Carmel took out her phone and placed a call to Charles Gagné. "Charles. Thanks for your email about our friend Todd. And yes, it could be very important. Tell me, has Richard Seaton called? Has he been asking for me?" She made a face at his reply. "Charles. He flew down from Makkovik to Goose Bay yesterday. He should have then been on a flight down to Montreal. Please check to see if he was and call me back. Thanks."

Emma was listening intently. "Is there something that's bothering you?"

"Yes and no," Carmel replied. "If there is, I'll let you know. So Richard was worried about having lost his computer. Did he say why? Did he have any specific reason to be worried?"

"Not really. Like I said, at first, he thought it was the Wi-Fi in our house."

Carmel remained silent. "Where do you live?"

Emma pointed up the hill. "The white house, at the top on the left."

"Do you live alone?"

"No. I live with an older couple, Rose and Johnny. They have a granddaughter who is a nurse called Sarah, but she's away just now. She works in Nain, and is married to a man named Josh. He works up north as well, even further up the coast. But I think I told you all of that when we met in Montreal."

"Some of it anyway. What work does Josh do?"

"Maintenance work. At a radar site."

"At a radar site?" Carmel looked at Emma closely. Again, a radar site! She could scarcely believe the coincidence. There had to be a reason.

"Yes. The one at Saglek. Josh says it's part of the North Warning System. They have radar sites all across the Canadian arctic. Six or seven of them are here in Labrador."

"So Josh does maintenance work at one of them?"

"Yes. At Saglek."

"Where's Saglek?"

"It's about an hour's flight north of Nain, at the start of the Torngats. They're the really high mountains in the north of Labrador."

"What is there at Saglek? Is there a village?"

"At Saglek? No. I've never been myself. Josh says there's a landing strip which the Americans built back in the days of the DEW line, some old buildings, one of those domes up on a hill with a whole lot of radar and radio gear in it, plus fuel tanks and a generator. Usually, there's no-one there but Josh. Josh and a lot of bears. He says there are polar bears everywhere. He has to be quite careful."

"It's military, the radar?"

"Yes, I think so. Surveillance radar, for missiles, planes, that sort of thing."

"I see. Tell me about Josh."

"Josh? Like I said, he's married to Sarah. It's been about a year now. He's just turned twenty-four and comes from Hopedale. He lost his parents when he was quite young. I've known him ever since he was in school. I was working as a teacher then and had him in my class. I really like him. He's a nice kid."

"Did you enjoy teaching?"

"Well, yes. I loved it, being with the children. All of that. I taught English, and a bit of Maths."

"How long did you teach?"

"Six or eight years."

"Is that all? What made you stop?"

Emma looked away. "I don't know. Maybe I'm just more of an outdoors type."

16

By now, Carmel was happy that she had come to Makkovik, and that she had been able to check Richard's story as far as coming up to Labrador to see Emma was concerned. Then there was the little matter of the swapped laptop. She would have to tell Sonny about that. She had even learned a bit about the radar sites in Labrador. So when Emma invited her home for a bite of supper, she accepted with good grace.

"Hop on," Emma said to her, pointing to a quad bike that was parked on the jetty, "and I'll show you the sights."

Carmel mounted the bike behind Emma, and they went up the hill past a scattered assortment of houses with a variety of skidoos, quad bikes and trailers parked outside. The road was bumpy, and a trail of dust spread out behind them.

At the top of the hill, they came to a neat wooden house with its back tucked into the trees. It was on one floor and had a shiny stainless steel stovepipe sticking up at the back, with smoke curling lazily out from the top. There were wooden steps leading up to the front porch, and Carmel could see a face appearing in one of the windows. "This is home," Emma said to Carmel as they dismounted. "Hello, Rose," she shouted. "Are you there?"

A tall Inuit woman, quiet and erect, her face and hands dark and weathered, came out to greet them. She was dressed simply in a heavy raw cotton tunic with long sleeves and an embroidery of purple and yellow flowers at the collar and the cuffs. Her hair was black streaked with grey and was tied up in a bun at the back of her head. She had a broad, intelligent forehead and her eyes were narrow and deep set. The nose was pronounced, long and straight, with a sharp ridge. She always seemed to be smiling, but it was a restrained, severe smile, if it was a smile at all. She gave Emma a slow hug and said something that Carmel couldn't understand. The two were talking in what seemed to be a mixture of English and Inuktitut. Emma was explaining Carmel's presence to Rose, and it took her a while. "Come on in," she finally said to Carmel.

There was a fire going in a cast-iron stove in the living room, and it threw off a lot of heat, as well as a delicious smell of softwood smoke. Carmel noticed a collection of photos on the wall. There was one of a young woman in her graduation robe wearing a mortarboard. That had to be Sarah. Another showed a young man with a small moustache, standing in front of a collection of derelict buildings. Presumably Josh.

Johnny Watt rose to greet them, a big man with a face that was more Scots than Inuit, although when you looked for a while, you could see both. He had been out in his boat checking his nets and had nothing to show for it. "Too bright," he grumbled, as he shook Carmel's hand.

"Make yourself comfortable," Emma said, as she pointed out the bathroom. Carmel made a quick visit and then continued to look around the room. She noticed a photo of Emma standing with another woman under some palm trees. Emma was clearly younger then, and the other woman was holding up a parasol that slightly shaded her face. "That's a nice picture of you," she said to Emma. "Where was that taken?"

"Somewhere down south," Emma replied. "About ten years ago."

Carmel peered at the picture. "You look really nice. Who's with you? Not a sister?"

"No. No. Just a friend."

"She looks a bit like Gloria, the woman who was travelling with Carlos."

Emma shrugged. "I wouldn't know. I never met her."

"What's it like, being in the police?" Emma asked, as they sat down to a supper of caribou stew. "Do you like it? How long have you been doing it?"

"I like it fine," Carmel told her. "Before that, I was in the army."

"Oh. Like my dad!" Emma was clearly impressed. They talked about that for a while, and Carmel told Emma about her years in the army, and about her two tours of duty in Afghanistan.

As they were washing up, there was a noise outside. An old man in a worn purple hockey jacket with Postville '57 written on the back came into the room, and he and Johnny sat down together by the stove for a game of checkers. Emma and Carmel found a spot on a sofa nearby, and Rose stood silently in a doorway watching them all, and wiping a pot with a dishtowel.

Johnny and his visitor bent over the checker board and started swapping stories about seal hunts and thin ice in accents that Carmel had the greatest difficulty understanding. The scene brought back pleasant memories of long winter nights back home on the farm when she was still living with her Mom and Dad.

"Yes, my son," she heard Johnny sigh, "I opened the trap of the tilt, and there they were, two of them staring right down at me. Wolves!"

"Must've smelled your socks, eh?"

"Or the smoke. I had a fire going, see. That was a rough trip. Oh man! Took me some time to get around the bay, patches of slob ice everywhere."

"That's where you need good dogs. When I had Blackjack, I could go anywhere. I remember one time I was out shooting seal. I saw one way out, all alone on the ice, a big square flipper, and I headed out with the dogs. Then we came to a crack in the ice and the team stopped. I threw Blackjack into the water and the other dogs followed. Right into the water, they went. I hung on to the komatik and pretty soon, we were up on the other side."

He advanced a checker with a smart smack. "Then I shot the seal. One shot, right through the head. Yessir, thems were the days!"

When finally she rose to leave, Carmel checked her phone. She had a text message from Gagné. He had gotten through to the airlines, and although Richard had been booked on a flight from Goose Bay to Montreal, he had never checked in. She told Emma.

"There's something going on, isn't there?" Emma said. "Something involving Richard and the radar sites. And those other people. You can't tell me; I understand that." She placed her hands on Carmel's shoulders and their eyes met. "Whatever it is, please keep him safe. You've got to. For me."

"I'll do my best, Emma. I promise you," Carmel replied. She felt good saying that.

That night, in her hotel room in Makkovik, Carmel had a down moment. She felt depressed. It was not something that was in her nature, to be depressed. But the efforts of the last several days, the complexity of the puzzle that was unfolding before her and the solitude of that hotel room had their effect.

"I'm with the Montreal police," she reminded herself. "My job is to find out who it was committed that murder down by the Lachine Canal. I am definitely not responsible for the safety of Canada's borders or the integrity of its radar sites."

She was operating way outside her area of comfort, or competence. But how could she back out now? She was in it, right up to the hilt.

One of Carmel's guiding principles was that if you came to an obstacle and didn't know what to do, you didn't hesitate, you didn't lose momentum. No. You went forward as if it wasn't there. Sometimes, obstacles appeared worse than they actually were. Sometimes, they just sorted themselves out all by themselves. "Keep going, Carmy," she said to herself. "Don't give up."

17

"Wake up," Richard said to himself several times. "Think!"

He tried blinking his eyes and taking deep breaths, but his brain remained fuzzy. His head ached terribly, and he was sitting on what felt like a wooden chair. Something was preventing him from moving his arms and his legs. It was like emerging from a nightmare, when the body is heavy and refuses to obey.

In addition, the place was dark and smelled dirty and damp. It made him feel claustrophobic. "Where the fuck am I?" he asked. A feeling of panic started to mount within him.

He gradually realised that his hands were bound together behind his back, and he clenched and reopened his fingers several times, trying to bring back the circulation. He tried to free his hands, but they were tightly bound. He tried to move his feet. They were attached as well. Then, the pain came to him, at his wrists mostly, but also in his ankles and his back. It was so bad that when he moved only slightly, he felt nauseous.

Even as he was trying to pull himself together, to

understand what was happening, he heard a muffled noise somewhere out in the darkness ahead of him. From slightly above came a feeble ray of light. He waited, his head aching more than ever, his senses dulled.

A voice came out of the semi-darkness. It sounded vaguely familiar, and he tried to place it. He heard it again, this time closer by. For a moment, he even hoped that it might be someone come to free him and help him get out of that place.

Then he knew. It was Todd's voice, soft and silky. He remembered it from the ride they had given him on the morning of the murder. Perhaps there was a connection between what was happening to him now and the murder of his half-brother Carlos. His heart froze.

"Hello, Richard," the voice said. "How are you doing?"

He then remembered being forced into a car at the airport terminal. It came back to him, the knee slamming viciously into his back, the cold cloth clamped over his nose and mouth, his struggle to resist. He had heard that voice at that time as well. Something like, "Easy on him, Rupert."

A bright light came on, dazzling his eyes so that he wanted to close them. It seemed to come from a lamp placed on a table a few feet in front of him. The profile of a man then pulled up a chair and sat down in front of him. Richard stared at him through the glare. He was wearing thick glasses with a steel frame. His face was square, and several days' stubble bristled on his chin and above the thin lips. It was Todd.

A second person now made his appearance, not somebody Richard could recognise. He was short and had a bald head that was curiously shaped, like a round ball. He was holding a laptop in his hands. Richard saw his firm's logo on the cover. It was his own laptop, the one he had lost in Montreal. He struggled to understand why this man should have it.

"This is Valery," Todd said. He and the other man exchanged a few words, in a language that sounded Slavic, possibly Russian.

Richard tried to concentrate. What were Todd and Rupert doing in Labrador? Why had they grabbed him at the airport and brought him to this place? How come they had his office computer? Who was this other man, the one with his laptop? What was the connection with the murder of his half-brother Carlos? The only thing he could think of was that the whole thing could have something to do with the radar sites that he had been working on, the ones in Labrador.

A woman emerged from the darkness. She was slim and looked familiar. She approached and gave him a sympathetic smile. It was Gloria. She passed behind him, and he could feel her hands on his wrists as she untied the cords which bound his hands. He could hear her breathing, and her hair brushed against the back of his head. "This will make you feel better," she said, as she pulled the cords away. He brought his hands forward and rubbed them together.

"We're really sorry, Richard," Todd started. "We want to ask you a few questions, that's all."

Gloria reached out a glass of water. "Here, Richard. You must be thirsty." He refused angrily, twisting his head to one side.

"How are you feeling?" Todd asked. Richard said nothing but gave him a blank stare.

"You know, of course, that your brother Carlos was killed last week," Todd continued. "We were very sorry to learn about it. Really. Our condolences."

Richard tried to swear at Todd, but his throat was so dry, all that came out was an ugly *Aaaargh*. Gloria reached out the glass of water, and this time he took it and had a long swallow. He returned the empty glass to Gloria and tried to clear his throat. "You bastards," he shouted in a voice he could scarcely recognise as his own. "Let me go!"

Todd just smiled. "Gloria thinks it was you who discovered the body. Is that right?"

Richard remained silent.

"You then called the police?"

"Fuck you!" Richard croaked.

Todd ignored him and repeated the question. "You called the police?"

Richard tried to collect his thoughts. Should he say nothing? Should he say yes? What would most likely get him out of there fast, in one piece? After all, they were brutal; they had killed Carlos. He nodded silently.

"Did they have you go down to the police station, ask you a whole lot of questions? Who was there? A man called Sonny Samuels? A woman called Carmel Roch?"

Again, he nodded.

"Anyone else?"

He shook his head. "No."

"Did they mention any names, people they felt might have killed your brother?"

He shook his head again. "No."

"Have you spoken to either of them since you came to Labrador?"

"No."

Todd leaned threateningly forward. With his right hand, he seized Richard by the chin. "You'd better be sure. You have spoken with Ms Roch, haven't you?" He gave Richard's head a savage shake and spat the words in his face. "I want to be absolutely clear. If you lie to us, just once, you'll never get out of here alive. Never! Do you understand?"

Richard struggled to answer. His jaw felt almost dislocated. "No, I haven't spoken with her," he shouted. Strange thoughts started to flash through his head. Were they going to torture him to death? Was he about to die? Could this really have something to do with the radar sites? Perhaps they had made a mistake. Perhaps they thought he was someone else.

Todd and Valery exchanged a few words, and then Valery opened the laptop. Holding it forward so that Richard could see what he was doing, he keyed in a number of entries, and found the folder containing the specs and drawings for the radar sites that Richard had been working on. Richard's heart sank. So it was the radar sites, after all.

"Which ones are for Saglek?" Todd asked. Richard remained silent.

Gradually, he recalled that the drawings were for a number of different radar sites, and that the actual locations weren't named; they were only identified by a number.

Todd repeated his question. "Which ones are for Saglek?" He then turned around. "Rupert," he called. "Come join us."

Rupert came quickly forward, and a moment later, Richard's left arm was twisted behind him and upwards, and he felt an excruciating pain in his left shoulder.

"Saglek?" Todd repeated. Rupert pulled his arm even higher.

Richard let out a yell. The pain was terrible. Rupert let go, and the arm dropped like a limp rag down along his side.

Todd looked at the screen of the laptop. "1621. Where's that?" Richard hesitated. Rupert stepped forward, his fist raised, but Todd restrained him. "Where's 1621, Richard?"

"Saglek is 1274," he muttered.

"Thanks," Todd said, as Valery flicked through the files looking for the right drawings. Richard immediately regretted his answer. Perhaps he should have given the wrong number. But it was too late now.

Valery was saying something to Todd and pointing to something on one of the drawings. Richard could see that it had something to do with the transmission antennas at Saglek. "What's that for, Richard?" Todd asked. "That cable connection, there?"

Richard hesitated once more, and Rupert's fist slammed into the side of his head, knocking both him and his chair flying. He lay there on the floor, his ear ringing. He tried to fake unconsciousness.

Rupert picked him up by the shoulders and put him back on the chair. He slapped Richard twice in the face. "Wake up," he barked, "or I'll punch you again, only a lot harder."

"You'd better help us," Todd added, "or he'll end up killing you."

Again, he hesitated, and another punch landed on his face. This time, it landed on the side of his jaw, and he really did pass out. For how long, he couldn't tell. When he came to, he was alone in the dark, bound once more hand and foot, and nauseous with the pain.

"Emma," he silently prayed. "Emma. Save me. Get me out of here. Somehow."

18

After spending a night at the hotel in Makkovik, Carmel flew back to Goose Bay. Just as she was checking in to her hotel there, her cellphone rang. It was Emma.

"Carmel, is that you? Any news of Richard?" Carmel told her that there were no new developments.

"There's something going on, Carmel. Someone called here at nine o'clock this morning and Johnny answered. He asked for Josh, the caller did. Said he was calling from Goose Bay." Emma sounded worried.

"Did he say who he was?" Carmel asked.

"No. Johnny says he had a foreign accent, not like people speak around here. Johnny told him Josh was up at Saglek, and wouldn't be back for a while yet. The man hung up. Carmel. Who do you think that was?"

"I don't know, Emma, but there could be a connection." She didn't want to alarm Emma unduly, but it certainly sounded like there was. "Thanks for telling me," she added, and they rung off.

It was time to call Sonny again. "Several developments, Sonny. Have you got a moment?"

He sounded cautious. "Yes."

"I was in Makkovik yesterday," she started, "and saw Emma. Richard was there with her for a while, but he had already returned to Goose Bay."

"Yes. Charles told me. And he never caught his flight to Montreal. Any further news of his whereabouts?"

"No. But he seems to be up here somewhere. One thing I learned yesterday from Emma is that Richard has lost his laptop." She went on to tell Sonny how she thought that had happened.

"So now, they can access all his files."

"If they have his laptop, yes they can."

"That's not very good!"

"No, it isn't."

"There's something else, Sonny. When I was in Makkovik, Emma told me about a young Inuit called Josh. She knows him very well. He lives in the same house as her, with his wife Sarah."

"Right."

"Josh works on a radar site. He lives up there, all alone, during the summers, doing maintenance work. The name of the site is Saglek. It's on a fjord called Saglek Fjord."

"Spell that name for me, please. The fjord."

"S A G L E K. Ends in a 'K'." She waited for a moment. "Emma called me just a moment ago. A man—she doesn't know who—called their house this morning, trying to reach Josh. He had a foreign voice. In any case, that's what the person who took the call said. So you see, suddenly, out of the blue, a stranger wants to speak to Josh, to find out where he is, and calls the number, doesn't identify himself, and rings off."

"Who do you think the caller was?"

"One of these people, for sure. After all, they're up

here for a special reason. They want to get Valery onto a radar site. I think we can assume that radar sites are fenced off, that there is security. Having Josh to help get them onto a site could make a big difference.”

“If you’re right, we now know where they’re headed. To Saglek. Where is it anyway?”

“Emma described it for me. Way up the coast, beyond Nain. No more trees. No villages. High mountains. Bad weather. Polar bears. And a radar site.”

“How do you get there?”

“By plane, I guess. There’s a landing strip the Americans built a long time ago for the DEW line.”

“Do you think these people have their own plane?”

“I haven’t a clue. But there are charter operators all over the place.”

“How many of them are there? Todd. Rupert. Valery. Gloria. That would take a fair-sized plane.”

“And there might also be Richard. Yes. It would either take a Twin Otter, or one of the larger helicopters.”

Sonny changed subjects. “I’m going to Ottawa tomorrow. I have an appointment with someone I know in the RCMP.”

“Don’t abandon me. Don’t forget, I have a murder to solve.”

He laughed. “No. I won’t. I promise. Stay safe.” He hung up.

After a shower, Carmel took a long walk around town, stopping along the way for a sandwich at the usual restaurant. “Do I have a plan?” she asked herself. She had to admit that she did not. Eventually, she returned to her room and updated the notes she was keeping on her computer.

At around five o’clock that afternoon, she glanced out the window of her room. Below her in the hotel’s parking area were a number of heavy duty and mid-sized pickup trucks and minivans, all generously coated with dust. She thought that they probably belonged to people working at the Muskrat Falls hydroelectric project, or to prospectors returning from the north, loaded with their rock samples.

She noticed Anand, the delivery man from the pizza restaurant, crossing the parking area with one of his pizza boxes. It was not the first time she had seen him down below with a delivery. A thought suddenly came to her. Could it be that the pizza had been ordered by Richard, and that Richard was holed up just fifty feet away from her? Or, for that matter, Todd, Rupert and Valery?

She left her room and hurried down the stairs just in time to intercept Anand before he could make his delivery. "Hello, Anand," she greeted him. "You never stop. I see you in the restaurant; I see you out here. You are everywhere!"

He gave a foolish shrug, and tried to get by her, but she blocked his way, at the same time noting the suite number that was written on the box. "I was at your restaurant earlier today. Don't you remember me?" He gave her a blank look. "Tell me, Anand. How many takeouts do you think you do in a day?"

He seemed increasingly confused. "Oh. Quite a few. Maybe ten or fifteen."

"Are they always to the same people?"

"No. It varies."

"I guess it's handy for them, not having to go to the restaurant all the time. I should try it sometime."

"Sure. You should."

He started to move forward again, and Carmel stuck her hands out and grabbed the pizza box. "I'll take it up for you," she said. "We're travelling together." She left him there, protesting feebly, and bounded up the stairs two at a time, feeling the adrenalin rising within her. You never knew! She reached the end of the balcony, checked the number on the door, and knocked. "Takeout," she called.

From inside, she could hear the sound of someone getting out of a chair. She waited expectantly. After what seemed like quite a while, the door swung partly open. She took a step forward and paused in the doorway before entering the room. "Takeout," she repeated.

A man stood inside the door, with his back partly turned towards her, and a twenty-dollar bill in his hand.

19

As she stood in the doorway, Carmel felt an unusual tightness in the throat. She was prepared for the possibility that the man in the room was a total stranger, in which case she would hand over the pizza and get out of there as quickly and as elegantly as possible. She was also prepared for trouble. Her body was tense, ready to react if there was any threat of violence. "I'll just throw the whole thing at him, box and all," she said to herself, looking down at the pizza in her hands. "It's still hot. That would slow him down." She glanced behind her to make sure that the door was open.

She took a rapid but careful look into the room. It was unexceptional, much like her own. She could see two large double beds, one that had been occupied, as the covers were thrown back, and the other, with a suitcase and neat stacks of clothing on top of it. A cooking counter lay along the right-hand wall, and through an open door on the left she could see into the bathroom.

She examined the man in front of her. From the back, he looked to be of medium stature, not as tall as she remembered Richard to be. Nor did he look like he could be Rupert or Todd. Her heart fell. "Oh my God," she said to herself. "I've screwed up. This guy isn't Richard, or any of the others. I'm going to have to hand over the box and clear out fast!" He slowly turned to face her, and her initial reaction of disappointment quickly turned into one of amazement.

He hadn't shaved for several days, and his cheeks were covered with a blonde stubble. His face was that of an overgrown schoolboy, with round open eyes and a tangle of curly blonde hair on top. He was wearing purple velvet pants and a rumpled white linen shirt.

"Carmy. You've hit the jackpot!" she said to herself in triumph. "This is Carlos!"

She couldn't believe her good luck, and her mind raced ahead. What were her priorities? What more did she wish to learn about the murder, its circumstances, the victim? More generally, what was Carlos doing in Goose Bay? Was he working with the others? Could he help her find Richard?

"Just standing in for Anand," she explained with a businesslike seriousness, stepping into the room and holding the pizza box out for him.

"Thanks," he said, looking suspiciously at her, and taking the box. He placed it on the table and reached out the twenty-dollar bill. "Keep the change."

"Thank you," she said, taking the note. "I'll give it to Anand." She smiled, feeling slightly awkward in her assumed role as pizza courier.

"Well, are you going to leave?" He looked at her impatiently, almost angrily.

Carmel had to find an excuse to stay, to start a conversation. "You should come down to the restaurant sometime," she said. "There are other things to eat—

PIZZA

sandwiches, curry..."

He cocked his head to one side, like a heron would as it stared at its reflection in the water. "You're phony," he said. "And you have an accent. You must be from Quebec."

Carmel didn't flinch. "Yes. I'm from Montreal." She smiled at him. "You have an accent too. Where are you from?"

"What's that to you?" He looked angrily at her. "Who are you, anyway? What are you doing here?"

"My name's Carmel. Yours?"

"Look, Carmel, if that's really your name. Enough's enough. Leave." He gestured towards the door. "Out!"

"OK. I'll go, Mr...What did you say your name was?"

He almost growled. "Rolf. My name is Rolf. Now go."

Carmel couldn't believe her ears. Not only had she found Carlos Antana, presently standing in front of her in flesh and in blood. In addition, he was pretending to be someone else, someone called Rolf. What possible reason could he have for doing that? And why Rolf? Could that be the name of the man who looked like him, and who had been murdered in his place? Had she just learned the murdered man's name? Was it Rolf? This was a major breakthrough, the kind you always hope for and rarely get!

She looked carefully at him. She didn't have the impression that she was in the presence of a dangerous person. "He's more of a boy scout than a Jack the Ripper," she said to herself. Sitting down on a chair by the window, she placed her forearms on the table. That way, he would be able to see that she wasn't armed. "Let's have a talk," she said, giving him a prudent smile, and laying the twenty-dollar bill across the table from her.

He took the pizza box over to the cooking counter and slowly returned. "Who are you, anyway?" he asked, as he stood in front of her. "What's your game?"

"My name is Carmel Roch. I'm with the Montreal Police."

A shadow crossed his face. "I might have guessed." His eyes narrowed. "You're a long way from Montreal. What brings you to Goose Bay?"

Carmel slowly rose to her feet and looked him in the eye. "Mr Antana. Someone was murdered in Montreal about ten days ago. In the hallway of a condo down by the Lachine Canal. The condo where you were staying. That's what brings me here." She watched closely to see what his reaction would be. Was he going to stop pretending that he was a man called Rolf?

His face went beet red, and he looked at her angrily. He pointed emphatically towards the door. "Madame," he said. "You've got the wrong person, and I don't know what you're talking about. Get out."

She stood her ground. "I was the first police officer to arrive on the scene. We have compared blood types." She pointed at him. "We know for a fact that it wasn't you, Carlos Antana, who was killed."

"That's..." He stopped, looking bewildered. "Blood types?" he muttered with a frown. "What blood types?" he asked.

"That of the dead man, obviously, and the one shown for you in a medical report we got from the police in Nassau." He stared at her. Now she had his attention!

"Look," he said. "You're just guessing, and you're talking nonsense. In addition, you're making me very angry."

Carmel pressed on. "What's more, we could see that the murdered man looked like you. That was no coincidence. It was Rolf who was murdered, wasn't it?"

"Please, Ms...." He stopped.

"Roch," Carmel said. "Pronounced ROCK. Spelled R O C H .

There was a long pause in their conversation. Carlos was clearly undecided—should he cooperate with her, or not? Carmel sensed that if she persisted in asking questions bearing directly on the murder, he would simply refuse to answer. She had to take a new approach.

She sat down again and leaned back in the chair, trying to look as though she was making herself comfortable and intending to stay for a good long while. "I have gotten to know your brother Richard. He was the one who discovered Rolf's body and who called us at the police station. He seems a very decent person."

He said nothing. He must have realised that by agreeing with her, he would be abandoning the pretence that he was Rolf. However, he was now looking at her with a mixture of curiosity and respect. "Good try," he seemed to be saying.

"I'm worried for Richard's safety," she continued. "I have my reasons. Couldn't we please have a little talk?"

Slowly, Carlos went to the chair on the other side of the table from her and sat down. A change had taken place between them. He was now accepting that she could stay, at least for a while.

"Did you know that Richard came up here to Labrador recently?" Carmel asked. "He has become good friends with a woman named Emma Sinclair. He was staying with her, in Makkovik."

He nodded silently.

"She went to your show with him."

He smiled, just a little. "Yes. I think I saw her there." Carmel relaxed. Things were moving her way.

"I visited Emma just a day ago, in Makkovik. I wanted to talk again with Richard, but he had come back here, to Goose Bay. So we missed each other. Do you know where he is now?"

"No." The answer was peremptory. Too much so, Carmel thought. Carlos must also have realised this as well, and looked uneasy. "Why would I know that?" he finally asked.

Carmel made a dismissive gesture with her hands. "It's just that I'm afraid Richard may be in danger, and would like to prevent anything happening to him. That's why I want to locate him."

Carlos said nothing. Carmel examined his face. It was mild and generous, not hard and selfish. She remembered Richard telling Sonny and her that Carlos sponsored foster children in different parts of the world, including one in Labrador. She decided to take a stab in the dark.

"Emma has a young friend named Josh, who works up at the radar site at Saglek. She tells me that yesterday, someone was trying to reach him by phone, calling from Goose Bay. Was that you?"

She looked closely at Carlos' face. You could almost say that it betrayed itself by not reacting. "You called, asking for him, didn't you? Why did you want to get in touch with him?"

Carlos looked angrily at her. "What makes you think I tried to get in touch with him?"

Carmel sought to placate him. "I know that you have supported a number of schools and foster children in the past, and I admire you for that."

"Who told you that?" He frowned.

"Gloria did. You also said so to Richard. Josh needed help when he lost his parents, and you gave it to him, isn't that true?"

Carlos no longer knew what to admit and what to deny. "Yes," he finally said. "I tried to speak to Josh. We have kept in touch over the years, not often, but occasionally, and I was hoping to meet him in person this trip. I had no idea that he had some connection with Richard's friend Emma."

"No. It seems to be quite a coincidence, but Labrador is a small place, so perhaps, it is not all that surprising." Carmel leaned forward in her chair. "Do you think Richard and Josh would agree to cooperate with the others, with Todd, Rupert and Gloria?"

Carlos looked angrily at her. "You're asking me about things...I have nothing to do with."

She disregarded his denial. "What worries me is that if either Richard or Josh isn't willing to cooperate with them, his life may be in danger. Your business partner Rupert Marsham can be exceedingly violent. And what do you think of Todd? He strikes me as being a very dangerous individual."

Carlos was looking tired, and more than a bit self-defensive. "I don't know that much about Todd. I've heard about him, mainly through Rupert, but I have never actually met him in person."

"Not even once, with Richard? In a car with Gloria driving, on the morning of the murder?"

"No." His denial was convincing. Carmel had already guessed that on that occasion, it had been Rolf in the car, pretending to be Carlos. Carlos wearily rubbed his forehead with his right hand. "You know a lot, don't you?"

"There are gaps. Gaps you could help fill in."

"If I help you fill them in, what will happen next?"

"I will do all in my power to make sure Richard is safe. Josh too." She looked at Carlos expectantly. "Surely, we share that goal." He nodded. "So, where is Richard, then? Tell me."

Carlos seemed to be thinking hard now. He was probably trying to decide just how much he could trust Carmel. "He's probably with the others. The people you mention. Todd, Rupert and Gloria. I don't know where, though. Somewhere up here."

"Is he with them voluntarily?"

"Possibly not."

"Why are you up here?"

He rubbed his forehead again. "Old scores. I have one or two old scores to settle."

Carmel smiled for an instant. For her, an old score had something to do with the previous hockey season. "What do you mean by that? Is it that there is someone you would like to get even with?"

"Precisely."

"And who is that?"

"That would be telling, wouldn't it?"

He was getting visibly impatient. He started to get up and then sat down again. "There is one thing I must ask of you. Then, I'd like you to go."

"What is it? If I can help you, I'll do so."

"Keep your lips closed. With Rupert and the others, if ever you run into them. It's important to me. Very important."

"Keep my lips closed about what?"

"About me. That I'm here. Particularly, the fact that I'm Carlos, not Rolf."

Carmel took a deep breath. "I'll do that. You can count on it."

He looked relieved and rose from his chair. His face had relaxed once more, and with an impish grin, he retrieved the twenty-dollar bill from the table. Carmel followed him to the door and held out her hand. A good handshake would seal the pact between them.

There was a moment of hesitation, and Carmel worried that the pact was stillborn. Then, to her astonishment, he took her hand and raised it lightly to his lips. "You're damn good at your job," he murmured. She was stunned. A kiss on the hand. Her first time ever! Like in the movies. A moment later, she had been ushered out onto the balcony of the motel, and his door had closed behind her.

20

"Sonny. You'll never believe this!" She glanced rapidly at her watch. It was already half-past nine. "I've found Carlos. We had a long talk." Carmel was sitting on the bed in her hotel room, her laptop open beside her. It contained the notes she had made immediately after she left Carlos. "Sorry to call so late," she added. "You're probably going to bed."

"Not exactly. Don't forget there's a one hour time difference. That's exciting news! Where did you see him?"

"Right here. He's been hiding in the motel where I'm staying, three doors down the hall. Well, it's not a hall, really. More like a balcony. Near me, in any case." Carmel proudly described how she had taken the pizza box from Anand and presented herself at the door of the room where Carlos was staying. She could hear Sonny laughing. "Would I have thought of that?" he asked her. "Probably not."

Carmel summarised her conversation with Carlos. "At first, he didn't want to say who he was. Then, he wanted me to believe he was a man called Rolf. I guessed, I think correctly, that Rolf was the name of his look alike, the man who was murdered."

"You think Carlos has been pretending to be this man Rolf ever since the murder occurred?"

"Yes. It seems so."

"That's unusual. Why would he do that?" Sonny paused. "Perhaps this guy Rolf is very important, and the murder was arranged so that Carlos could take his place and impersonate him."

"Yes. Or perhaps it's the other way around. Perhaps Carlos is, as you put it, very important, and Rolf was going to take his place, but got murdered in the process."

"That somehow seems more likely," Sonny agreed. "And now, you say, Carlos is pretending to be Rolf. That means that he must have some feeling for what Rolf was like. Maybe he knew him from the Bahamas. I'll call them down there, see what I can learn. Too bad you don't have a second name. Are you really sure that Carlos is pretending to be Rolf?"

"Yes. He told me so himself."

"But why? Why would he pretend to be Rolf?"

"It can't be to fool us. I told him that we have compared blood types and know that the dead man wasn't him, but somebody else. And at the end of our conversation, he specifically asked me to keep my lips closed, not to tell Rupert and the others that he is Carlos, and not Rolf. So if he is pretending that he is Rolf, it must be for their benefit, not ours."

"They are the ones he wants to fool."

"Exactly."

"And do we think that the others don't know who was murdered? That they think Carlos is dead, not Rolf?"

"Yes, I suppose so. That would follow from what Carlos was saying."

"Except maybe Gloria. You had the impression that Gloria knows, and that the purpose of her visit was to see if we knew." Sonny reflected on that for a while. "And you say that Carlos is up in Labrador, hiding out in your motel."

"Definitely. Three doors away. He also knows that Rupert and the others are up here as well. He as much as told me. But he's not with them, and doesn't want them to know where he is."

"If, as you think, the others are involved in some kind of plot to take a Russian spy onto one of the radar sites, they must be in hiding as well, somewhere near where you are."

"That's right. With their white Honda. I think they probably have Richard with them as well." There followed a long silence, broken by the sound of Sonny muttering to himself. Carmel could almost see him sitting there, with a frown of concentration on his face, turning it all over in his mind. She took the opportunity to stuff another pillow behind her back.

"The plotters wanted Carlos dead," Carmel continued. "They sent Rolf to kill him. Afterwards, their intention was that Rolf, who looked like Carlos, would pretend he was Carlos."

Sonny had his Eureka moment. "They even brought that body bag with them! That way, they could remove the body, and there would never be the suspicion that someone had been murdered. Rolf would carry on as Carlos, that was all."

"That's right." She paused. "Sonny. My theory is as follows. I think they wanted Carlos to bring Richard into their plot, and Carlos refused. Maybe he even threatened to denounce them. So they decided to kill him and replace him with a look alike, one that they had waiting in the wings, just in case. Somehow, it went wrong, and the look alike, who we know was called Rolf, got murdered instead."

"Perhaps by Carlos, who saw him coming."

"Perhaps."

"So now, Carlos is carrying on as Rolf. Why would he be doing that? What's his game?"

"I think he is playing a waiting game, and a double game. When I asked him why he was up here in Labrador, he said he had an old score to settle. I took it to mean that he wanted revenge."

"On whom?"

"Probably Rupert. There are several possible reasons. There might have been something about the way Rupert acquired a half interest in the theatre building. Rupert may have been milking the night club for cash. There is also the way Rupert treats everyone, including Gloria, like dirt. Possibly Rupert was present at the attempt to kill Carlos the other day at the condo. Yes. My guess is that Carlos wants to get even with Rupert."

"And how will he do so?"

"He'll let them go up to the radar site, have the RCMP show up at the last moment and arrest everybody, and Rupert will spend the rest of his life in a prison somewhere in Canada. That's how."

Sonny thought that through for a while. "That sounds convincing. So he doesn't want them stopped. He wants them caught."

"Precisely."

"And you don't think he's in cahoots with them?"

"No. I don't. He told me he'd never met Todd in person. I find that credible. And don't let's forget there's Valery. He never mentioned him. He has several reasons for disliking Rupert, rather than wanting to plot with him.

And I just don't think Carlos is the type to flirt with spies. Also, if he was plotting with them at this late stage, I think they would all be staying together."

"How would Carlos even know that the others are up in Labrador just now?"

Carmel hesitated. "He must be in some sort of contact with them, all the while pretending he's Rolf, of course. He has probably persuaded them that it's safer for them all if he stays physically apart, for the time being."

"So as far as the plotters are concerned, there are five of them: Todd, Rupert, Gloria, Valery, and, in a certain sense, Rolf."

"Yes. And Carlos is a sort of counter-plotter. Gloria is perhaps a special case. She has always seemed to me to be close to Carlos, and an unlikely collaborator with Rupert, even if she is his wife."

"Maybe, but if, as you think, she's originally from the Ukraine, she probably speaks Russian. Like Valery. And probably like Todd as well."

"Good point." Carmel glanced at her notes. "Sonny. I have something to say about why Rolf is important to the plotters."

"Let's hear it."

"I told you before about Josh, who does maintenance work up at the radar site at Saglek. I think they want Rolf to come with them, pass himself off as Carlos, and convince Josh to let them on to the site.

"Why would this Josh be persuaded by Rolf?"

"It so happens that Carlos used to give money to boys in need, in various parts of the world, through some sort of fostering arrangement. Gloria told me so, and Carlos confirmed it. It turns out that Josh was one of the recipients."

"This same Josh?"

"Yes. Yesterday, Carlos tried to get in touch with him. He didn't really say, but I think he wanted to warn Josh to stay in a safe place when the fun starts at Saglek."

Sonny was still trying to catch up with Carmel's reasoning. "So they think Rolf will come to Saglek with them, pretend he's Carlos, and persuade Josh to let them onto the radar site."

"That's right."

"And what's preventing them from going on up to Saglek right away?"

"Nothing, apart from the fact that they are waiting for Rolf to appear. Perhaps Carlos has yet to talk to the Mounties and set the trap. Then, does he plan to actually go with them, still pretending he is Rolf? I can't say. I suppose they intend to fly in. They may just be waiting on the weather."

"Shouldn't you be a bit more suspicious of Carlos, Carmel? He may have told you a pack of lies."

"No, I think I'm on the right track. There's one thing that helps. He seems to be genuinely worried for Richard's safety, and for that of Josh. He knows that I am as well."

"Where is Richard anyway? Have you learned anything new?"

"I certainly have. Carlos seemed to confirm that he is being held, against his wishes, by the plotters. In fact, I'm very worried for Richard."

"They have his computer. Perhaps they don't need him any more."

"On the contrary, perhaps they need him to get into the files on his computer."

They both fell silent. "Anything else, Carmel?"

"No. That's just about it. I can't think of anything else right now. What about your trip to Ottawa? How did that go?"

"Badly or not so badly, depending on your point of view. The man I wanted to see wasn't free, and I met with a younger officer who said very little and took a lot of notes. I haven't heard from them since. Probably just as well."

With that, they ended their call. "Keep in touch," Sonny said, "and for God's sake, play it safe and stay out of trouble."

Speaking with Sonny had done Carmel a lot of good. It had enabled her to organise her thoughts, to find a place for more and more of the pieces of the puzzle. She slid down into her bed, pulled the covers up over her head, and had a good night's sleep.

When she got up the next morning and looked down the balcony towards Carlos' room, there was a laundry cart outside the door and two maids were changing the bed. Carlos had checked out. He was gone. In a way, Carmel was happy. That meant that at last, things were on the move!

21

Carmel's phone buzzed. "Hi, Carmel. It's Emma."

"Emma! Where are you?"

"On the ferry from Makkovik. Any news of Richard?"

"No. I'm afraid not."

"Me neither. Carmel, I'm getting really worried. I can't just stay there at home, waiting for something to happen. We've got to find him."

"Is that why you've come?"

"Yes. I know my way around Goose Bay better than you do. Perhaps I can help."

Carmel thought for a moment. Emma had a point. A bit of help might be good. "Do you want me to meet you? I could do that. When do you arrive?"

"In an hour or so."

"Okay. Wait for me down at Otter Creek. I'll come get you." She threw everything into her bag, checked out of the hotel and drove down to the ferry wharf at Otter Creek. When she arrived, the ferry was already disgorging its cargo of passengers, vehicles and containers, and Emma was standing to one side looking down the road for her.

She threw her bag in the back of Carmel's car and got in.

"Am I ever glad to see you!" she said to Carmel, leaning over and giving her a kiss on the cheek.

"Where do we go?" Carmel asked, as the car pulled away.

"First, let's go to my house in North West River. If that's okay with you."

"Where?"

"North West River. See that stop sign? Turn there. To the right." Emma leaned over to fasten her seat belt. "I have a small house there. It used to belong to my parents. Which hotel are you staying at?"

"Nowhere right now. I checked out."

"Good! Then you can stay with me. There's a sofa bed in the living room. Tell me what you've learned."

Carmel saw no alternative but to mention that she had met Carlos. "Emma. It's become very complicated. You see, that wasn't Carlos at all who was murdered in Montreal. Carlos is still alive and well. The murdered man was somebody else."

Emma stared out the window. "Surely that can't be," she said thoughtfully. "Richard told me the dead man was Carlos."

Carmel was surprised at her reaction. "Different blood types," she explained.

"I see." Emma sounded puzzled. "I know nothing about blood types. You mean that the dead man had a different type from that of Carlos? Can you be sure?"

Carmel had to think about that. There could always have been a mistake somewhere. "Pretty sure. Besides," she added. "I've now met Carlos, and I'm pretty clear that it was him."

"Where was he?"

"Actually, he was staying at the same hotel as me.

Here in Goose Bay."

"Oh. I see."

They drove on in silence. For a moment, Carmel asked herself if she could have made a mistake, if the Carlos she had met the previous day wasn't really Carlos at all. She decided that it couldn't be so. Not the way he looked. Not the way their conversation had gone. She was surprised that Emma hadn't reacted more positively to the news that Richard's half-brother was still alive.

"What about Richard then?" Emma finally asked. "Where do you think he is?"

"I hate to say so, Emma, but Carlos told me that he was possibly being held by the others."

"You mean the people who want to get onto a radar site? Gloria, Rupert, that bunch?

"That's right."

"You think they want to use Richard in some way?"

"Yes."

Emma shook her head. "The damn fools!"

"I also think I know which radar site. The one at Saglek."

Emma gasped. "Saglek! That's where Josh works. Oh Jesus!" She pulled out a handkerchief and blew her nose hard. Eventually, she settled down a bit, but Carmel could see that she was very upset.

They passed some scattered buildings and arrived at a long bridge. *Welcome to North West River,* a sign announced. At Emma's request, Carmel drove them into the village, and Emma purchased one or two things at a convenience store and made a quick visit to the Post Office to pick up her mail. A short while later, they had driven down a short gravel road and come to a quaint log cabin nestled in a clump of willows. A battered black pickup truck was parked on the lawn outside. "Welcome home,"

Emma said to Carmel, as she turned her key in the lock.

The house inside was small and cosy. The living room was panelled in spruce boards that had turned a mellow colour of nut brown, and there was a navy blue sofa, a table with two chairs, and two large windows, one of which looked down a certain distance to open water, whilst the other gave onto a stretch of lawn. In a corner was a cast-iron stove, and Emma took some firewood out of a large wooden box and started a fire.

She then pulled out a map of Goose Bay and spread it on the table, pointing at several places. "If I was them," she said to Carmel, jabbing a finger at the map, "I would find a secluded house, here, or here, or here. Do you think they are still driving the white Honda?"

"Yes. It's likely."

"Then let's drive around those places and look for one."

They returned to Goose Bay in Emma's truck and spent the next two hours looking for a white Honda. "They all look alike to me," Emma complained. "Hondas, Toyotas, Hyundais." She frowned. "I hope Josh is safe. I hope he comes home before they go up to Saglek. I'm really close to him, you know. When I was a teacher, he was my star student." She pointed to their right. "There's a white car, but it looks like a Chevy."

After they had been to all the places that Emma had in mind, they returned to North West River for a quiet supper. Later on, Emma made up the sofa bed for Carmel, and they both turned in.

The next morning, Carmel was the first to rise, and went to take a shower. She noticed how soft the water was when compared to Montreal. "I love your gel," she shouted over the top of the shower door to Emma, whose profile had appeared through the glass.

"I bought it in Montreal," came the reply. When Carmel came out of the shower, Emma was standing there. "My turn now," she said with a smile. "I hope you left me some hot water." She slipped by, handing Carmel a towel on the way.

Carmel started to rub herself down with the towel. She was puzzled. She had noticed a faded scar that ran across Emma's lower stomach. It was the sort of scar that could result from a C-section. Had Emma been married at some point in time? Had she given birth to a child that she had not so far mentioned? Once they were dressed, they sat down for breakfast, discussing how they would continue their search for Richard.

Carmel was about to pour herself a second cup of coffee when a noise outside caught her attention. It was hardly a noise, just the impression that something out there was moving, and moving in such a way as not to make any noise. She was sensitive to such things. Patrolling the roads and alleys of Kandahar had sharpened her instincts. She slipped out of her chair and turned towards the window. A moment later, a rock shattered the glass and fell at her feet.

She jumped back, startled, and shouted to Emma. "Watch out!" From beyond the window came a flash of light, and she could see flames. Grabbing a dish towel, she faced the window. A moment later, a bottle came sailing through the hole that the rock had made. A burning rag was wrapped around its neck, and there was the unpleasant smell of gasoline.

Carmel used the towel to catch the bottle before it could fall to the floor. Stepping towards the window, she threw the towel and the bottle back out the window, and the bottle landed at the feet of the man who had thrown it. He was tall, and had dark hair. She guessed it was Rupert.

There was an explosion of flame as the bottle broke,

followed by a howl of pain and fear. In a moment, he was rolling on the grass outside, trying desperately to extinguish the flames that were spreading up his legs. Carmel rushed out the door, picked up the towel, and threw it to him. "Use that, you dumb bastard."

All was urgency and violence outside, the flames, the smell of gasoline, the man rolling on the lawn. However, at the same time, all was deathly still. Too much so. Carmel didn't look—she didn't need to, and in any event she didn't have the time. She knew there was someone else out there. Someone behind her.

She quickly dropped to a low crouch. A second later, something heavy swung over the top of her head. It barely grazed her scalp. The only thing she felt at the time was the wind in her hair. She shifted her weight onto one leg and rapidly pivoted her body around and up, lashing out with the other leg as hard as she could. The instep of her foot caught her assailant on the left knee. There was a scream of pain.

"Run, Todd," Rupert was shouting. "Let's get out of here!" He started back towards the road, his pant legs smouldering and black with soot, and Todd limped heavily after him, swearing in some foreign language.

Emma was at the door of the house, shouting angrily after them. "You bastards! Who do you think you are, anyway?" She ran indoors to get a fire extinguisher, and rushing out again, sprayed the remaining flames on the lawn, as well as the lowest logs along the side of the house.

Carmel stood there, recovering her breath and looking anxiously down the road. She reached a hand to the top of her head. It was sticky, and there was a bit of blood. "Another centimetre, and I was a goner," she reflected.

## 22

Carmel stood at the door of the bathroom, sponging the top of her head with a damp towel. "You know, Emma," she said. "Those guys came on foot. They have to be hiding out somewhere close by."

Emma sat in a chair, fuming with anger, and looking at the pieces of broken glass scattered on the floor. "The bastards. What did they think they were doing?"

"They must have seen us somewhere yesterday, maybe in the village, and wanted to intimidate us, or worse."

"But why?" Emma asked. "Why?"

"Because they don't want us to stop them from going up to Saglek. Also, they're holding Richard, and they don't want us to try to rescue him." Carmel threw the towel on a chair. "Try to think where they could be. Are there any empty houses around here?"

"I don't know, but I have an idea," Emma said. She picked up her phone and dialled a number.

"It's Emma, Sadie. I have a question for you. Are there any strangers come to stay here in North West River? Just recently, in the last few days?"

Carmel waited as Emma continued the conversation. "Yes. A good-looking woman in her thirties. That's right. Three or four of them. Yes... That's the house at the end of the road, the one that's set back quite a distance in the trees? Who owns it, do you know? A rental? That's very helpful, Sadie. Got to go. Thanks a million." She turned to Carmel. "We've found them."

She described the house to Carmel. It was a two-bedroom bungalow set in some woods on the edge of the village, with only one or two neighbours, and none very close. It was not completely decorated, as the owner hadn't moved in yet.

Carmel looked at her watch. "After what happened here, they'll want to get out of there as soon as they can. We'd better act fast."

"Shouldn't we just call the police?"

"There may not even be enough time for that."

Emma held up a pair of steel-rimmed glasses. "I found these outside. Do you think..."

Carmel had a quick look. "They must be Todd's." She gave a short laugh. "Poor guy. He not only has a sore knee. He's also lost his glasses. You'd better give them to me."

She went to the door and checked outside, just in case Todd and Rupert were still around somewhere. "Tell me, Emma. How many roads are there out of North West River?"

"Just the one. The highway we took when we came here. It goes back to Goose Bay."

"Okay. We'll stop them there. Can we use your truck?"

"Of course."

"Here's what we're going to do. We'll wait for them somewhere along the highway. You can park with your truck on a side road, and when you see them coming, drive out into the middle of the highway and block it. At that point, I'll come up from behind with my car, and while I keep the four of them busy, you open the trunk of their car and pull Richard out. Put him in your truck and take the wheel. As soon as I join you, drive out of there fast."

Emma gave a whistle. "You think that'll work?"

"It's the best I can come up with, and we have to act quickly. Call your friend Sadie and ask her to pay them a visit. Right away. Have her go to the door and say that she's heard sirens and is afraid there's a fire somewhere. That'll make 'em move."

As soon as Emma had made the phone call to Sadie, they left the house, Emma in her truck and Carmel in the car. About seven kilometres out of North West River, Carmel pulled over, and they both got out and stood there in the middle of the road. There were no other vehicles in sight. A minor side road came in from their right. It was almost completely smothered by willows and alders, and deep in sand. "Back your truck in there, Emma, just far enough so you can still see what's coming. I'll return to the last curve and wait on the side of the road in amongst those bushes. When you see that they're past me, pull out and block the road. Okay?"

"Okay."

"Good luck! Keep your fingers crossed!" Carmel drove back up the road and parked in a spot half hidden under some alders. An occasional car or truck passed by, but for a while, things were pretty quiet. Finally, she saw what they were waiting for, and slumped out of sight in the driver's seat of her car.

The white Honda went by, driving very slowly. Carmel sat up again just in time to see the black pickup emerge from the side road and stop in the middle of the road. She pulled out and slowly caught up with the Honda.

The Honda suddenly accelerated. At fifty feet from

the truck, Gloria tried to fishtail it into a one-hundred-and-eighty degrees turn. Carmel saw what was happening and, pushing the accelerator to the floor, hung on to the wheel and prepared herself for the impact. In a squeal of tyres and a thud of metal, her car rammed the Honda from the side, smashing its driver's door. The shock was nasty, and the two cars were immediately caught in a tangle of metal in the middle of the road, with Emma's black pickup stopped ten metres beyond them.

Emma was the first to act. She jumped out of her pickup and ran over to the back of the Honda to open its trunk. "Richard!" she screamed.

Carmel could see Gloria struggling furiously to open the door of the Honda on the driver's side, but the collision had jammed it shut, so she started pushing Todd out on the other side. They both collapsed onto the pavement, and when they got up, he was limping badly.

Two other figures, Rupert and Valery, started to escape through the right-hand rear door of the Honda, and Carmel closed in on them, an improvised blackjack in her hand. She took a swipe at Rupert, who was the closer of the two, and caught him hard on the side of his head. He grunted and turned on her. "Bitch!" he shouted, as he tried unsuccessfully to grab her by the wind jacket. She hit him again and broke away. She then took a swing at Valery, but missed.

Rupert started towards the back of the Honda, where Emma was pulling Richard out of the trunk. "Stop her," he shouted. There followed a moment of indecision, with Rupert wanting to stop Richard from escaping and Gloria shouting at him and pointing to Emma's pickup. She had dragged Todd over to its far side and pushed him into the passenger's seat, and a moment later, Valery had piled into the back seat, carrying two small packsacks.

"Come on, Rupert, you asshole," Gloria screamed from the driver's door of the pickup, and at the last moment, Rupert turned away from where Emma was helping Richard off the road and leapt into the back of the pickup. With a roar of its engine, it disappeared down the road towards Goose Bay.

Emma was almost hysterical with joy. "They're gone!" she shouted, as she wrapped her arms around Richard. "We've got you!" She hugged him, kissed him, let him go, and then hugged him again. Several times. He was so dazed he could barely stand up. Carmel went over and gently cut through the twine binding his hands. Emma helped him hold his balance and rubbed his wrists to get the circulation going again.

The three of them sat down to rest on a log by the roadside. Richard put his arms around Emma's waist and buried his face in her lap. "You're so pale," she said, as she stroked his hair.

He looked up at her, and his voice trembled. "Thank God you came, Emma." Tears came to his eyes. "I had given up. I was expecting to die."

"This is Carmel," Emma said to him after a moment. "Montreal Police. Thank her, too."

Richard looked at Carmel, and slowly recognised her. "Yes. Carmel Roch." He took a deep breath. "Thanks," he said. "Thanks to both of you. You can't imagine..." He raised a hand to a dark bruise on the left side of his face, and touched it with his index finger. "Ouch!" he winced.

Carmel herself felt a deep sob coming. It sometimes happened to her, after moments of high excitement. She placed a call to the RCMP station and asked for Jim. "Last time I do this," she promised, once she had reached him and was explaining just where she was, and why.

She could hear his laugh. "Don't worry," he said. "I'm

gradually getting used to it. I never knew anyone from the Montreal Police before." He said he'd come right away, with a tow truck.

Carmel then called Sonny and gave him the news. He remained silent throughout and sounded unusually formal. "Carmel," he finally said. "First you chase a car through the town of Goose Bay. Then you crash into a car somewhere out on the highway. It's not very subtle, you know."

"They're not being very subtle either," she reminded him, "throwing Molotov cocktails through people's living room windows."

"Okay. But you're outside your jurisdiction, and you still haven't come any closer to knowing who committed that murder. I think it's about time you returned to Montreal."

Carmel almost swore sat him, she felt so angry. She was heading the investigation, not Sonny. She was risking her head in the process. Only twenty minutes before, she had taken on Todd, Rupert, Gloria and Valery, and she had won. Not bad. No-one was going to stop her now, not even Sonny. "I'll come when I'm good and ready," she said, and rang off.

A few minutes later, a RCMP cruiser appeared with a tow truck, and Jim got out. He greeted Emma, whom he already knew, and looked with concern at Richard, who remained pretty weak and pale. "Is he going to be alright?" he asked Carmel. She said she thought so.

The tow truck was still clearing the road when they headed back to Goose Bay. Jim left Emma and Richard off at the hospital, and took Carmel back with him to the station. During this time, they said very little to each other. "Where are things at in your murder investigation?" he asked once they had gained the privacy of his office.

"A lot has happened, Jim, but I'm not sure I'm very far ahead." She told him that a man named Rolf had been sent to murder Carlos in Montreal, and had ended up being killed instead. She related to Jim her conversation with Carlos, as well as her theory that Carlos was pretending to the others to be Rolf in order to lure them to Saglek and have the RCMP arrest them there at the critical moment.

When she had finished, she looked at Jim expectantly. He seemed ill at ease. "Carmel," he finally said. "What you are saying more or less corresponds to what the RCMP in Ottawa have been telling me. They know about the radar plot and they know about Carlos. They have also been in touch with Canadian Security, who are pretty excited and want Todd and Valery to be caught up at Saglek, red-handed. Apparently, a special team is on its way here from Ottawa."

Carmel sensed that her own investigation ran the risk of being sidelined. "What does that mean, Jim?"

"In Ottawa, Carmel, they want this to be a purely RCMP operation, without outside help, or interference. They think very strongly that you should stay away from Saglek." He sighed, and Carmel could see that he was embarrassed.

Her own face went red. "Now, I understand. My boss was on to me a moment ago, suggesting that I go back to Montreal. Someone has been putting the screws on him." She relaxed a bit. "I'll say this, Jim. You have been very straight with me, and I appreciate that. I want you to know that."

"Thanks, Carmel." Jim said, looking at her admiringly. "You deserve nothing less."

The two continued exchanging what information they each possessed. Carmel asked Jim how the plotters would likely go to Saglek. He said through Nain, which had a good airport.

"What's Nain like?"

"It's the most northern village in Labrador. About three hundred kilometres north of here. The population is mostly Inuit. From there, it would take Todd and his group about an hour to fly on up to Saglek."

"Why would they stop at Nain at all?" Carmel asked.

"They must have arranged for a plane to come get them. Possibly from Quebec somewhere. The pilot would normally want to refuel in Nain. Then there's the weather. It can be sunny in Goose Bay or Nain, and snowing hard in Saglek. There's a lot of bad weather in northern Labrador, and the landing strip at Saglek isn't equipped electronically, so a pilot needs at least fifteen hundred feet of cloud ceiling so he can see what he's doing."

The more they talked, the less Carmel could see what she should do. Jim was going to fly up to Nain the next day. Should she try to tag along? Her gut feeling was that she was closer to finding her murderer in Labrador than she would be in Montreal.

She decided she would go to Nain, at least. One last effort to get to the bottom of the mystery. She gave Jim a little smile. "Any chance of a ride up to Nain, Jim? Tomorrow?"

He thought about it for a moment. "The boys in Ottawa didn't say anything about your not going to Nain. They just don't want you up at Saglek."

That evening, Carmel had a text message from Emma. "Hi Carmel. Richard and I made it back to Makkovik. We're taking Walrus up to Nain. I'm worried for Josh."

23

"So this is Nain," Carmel thought.

A dog howled somewhere in the twilight, and several others joined in from other parts of the village. Apart from that, all was still. She walked up a gravel road, past a convenience store and then several houses, and finally arrived in front of the hotel. It was a small building, on two floors, and appeared to be deserted. There were no cars parked outside, just some heaps of scrap lumber and a rusty skidoo.

The flat white light of a television set flickered in a window near the entrance. She went cautiously up to the front door and peered inside. A man sat there alone in a big chair in the lobby, wrapped in a dark blue serge overcoat and chewing moodily on what looked like a stale ham and cheese sandwich. It was Carlos.

He had by now grown a short, light brown beard, and had a petulant, unhappy look on his face. As soon as he saw Carmel, he glanced away and pulled his coat more closely around his shoulders. After emptying his cup of tea, he carefully rewrapped the remaining bits of his sandwich in a scrap of cling film and stuffed them into a pocket of his coat. He rose, holding up the key to his room for her to see, mumbled "two", and headed for the stairs.

Carmel waited until she could no longer hear his footsteps on the floor above, picked up her bag, and followed him quietly up the stairs and along a short hallway. She paused at the door of room number two and tapped lightly. It opened at once, and Carlos stood there in silence, putting an index finger to his lips and inviting her to come in. When she had done so, he closed the door rapidly behind them. "The others arrived sometime today," he explained in a low voice. "We have to be careful. Very careful."

The room was bleak and needed a coat of paint. There were two single beds, a table and chair, plus a dresser.

"Brrr. It's cold in here," Carmel exclaimed softly as she sat down on a bed. She wondered how long Carlos would stick it out in the wilds of northern Canada.

"I hear you saved Richard," he said, as he stood there, looking at her. "Good going. Is he alright?"

"Yes. He's fine. He says he can't wait to see you again." This brought the semblance of a smile to his face.

"You've made yourself one or two enemies, you know," he said.

Carmel smiled in turn. "As they say, you can't make an omelet without breaking the eggs."

Carlos nodded his head in agreement, and after carefully putting what was left of his sandwich on the table, sat down on the other bed. He did not discard his overcoat. Carmel couldn't help but notice his socks. They were bright yellow and looked hand-knitted.

"I was hoping you'd stay in Goose Bay," he said.

"Why? What difference does it make to you?"

"What difference?" He hesitated. "I think that we both

know that Todd and the others are heading up to Saglek."

"Yes," she agreed.

"There's going to be a bit of excitement up there, and you could be one person too many."

"You mean that the Mounties will move in and arrest them? I know that. And incidentally, I haven't discussed your presence up here, or the fact that you are still alive, with Rupert or the others."

"Thanks. I knew I could trust you."

"That's what you want, isn't it? To get Rupert arrested. I have no problem with that."

"Yes, but the Mounties don't want you there. They want to arrest him and the others alone, not in conjunction with the Montreal police."

"Why?" She thought she already knew, but wanted to see what he would say.

"To retain total control and avoid screw-ups, I suppose. Also, to get all the credit. Think of it, otherwise... the headlines. 'RCMP seeks assistance of Montreal police to arrest famous Russian spy in northern Labrador.'"

Carmel smiled. "So you've heard about Valery." She paused to pull her wind jacket more closely about her shoulders. "Nobody is saying that I'll go to Saglek. I'm here in Nain, that's all for now. But I do have a murder to solve, and a murderer to arrest. That's why I'm here."

"I didn't do it; I can promise you that." He stood up. "Sorry, but I'm cold. Want a cup of tea?" He went over to a counter beside the door where an electric kettle stood on its stand. "Milk or plain?"

"Plain thanks. No sugar."

"So, why are you here, Carmel? What do you want of me?"

She smiled. "To ask you a few more questions. I thought we had a pact. I help you spring your trap, and you help me find my murderer."

"All right. I guess that's fair enough." He returned with two cups of tea and sat down.

"So who was Rolf?" she asked.

He waved a hand dismissively. "A two-bit actor off one of the cruise ships. He did stand-up comedy and impersonations, in between the bingo games and the step-dancing. One of Rupert's friends."

Carmel laughed. "How did he and Rupert meet?"

"They'd known each other, off and on. Rolf used to bring drugs into the Bahamas on the ships, the cruise ships. Rupert bought small quantities from him, for resale on the street, and later on, at our night club."

As he talked, Carmel studied his face. She found it an interesting face, the way the expressions came and went. Just now, he was looking severe.

"Rupert was then elbowed out of the way. A man everybody down there refers to as Mr Big came into the picture. He took over the trade and then brought Rupert back as one of his henchmen."

"Is Mr Big in some way involved in the plan to go up to Saglek?"

"He certainly is." He emptied his cup and took it back to the counter for a refill. "Last time we met, you asked me about Todd, the man whose knee you nearly broke in two. Well. Mr Big and Todd are pals. They see each other every winter, skiing in the Alps. From what I know, Todd lives somewhere in the Middle East, and does illegal arms deals. He's very cozy with Iran and the Russians."

"And Mr Big?"

"He's your normal high-class thug. He knew from Rupert about my ties to Richard and to Josh, and about the kind of work Richard does." Carlos leaned back and gestured with his hands. "I think they saw an opportunity to make a lot of money by getting a Russian spy onto a radar site in northern Canada. Mr Big agreed to provide Rupert and Gloria and to finance the operation. Todd's job was to get the Russians interested, and to bring the Russian spy to Canada."

"Let's move on to the moment when you all came to Montreal. Why come to Montreal?"

"That was Rupert's suggestion, but I was happy with the idea. After all, Montreal is my old home town. Also, I thought that it would be a good opportunity to see Richard again. At the time, I knew nothing of the other plan, the one having to do with the radar site."

"So you came to Montreal and put on the show. What role in the show did Rupert and Gloria play?"

"They didn't participate as performers. However, Rupert handled ticket sales, and Gloria organised the actors. She found the extras through a specialised agency in Montreal. She also took charge of setting things up beforehand, and cleaning up the mess the next day."

"Gloria is pretty important to you, isn't she?"

He smiled. "I don't know what you mean by that, but she sure is efficient."

"When did you first hear talk about the idea that you should all come up here, to Labrador?"

"Rupert had already mentioned it, even before we came to Montreal, but he made it sound like a possible side trip. We could have Richard show us around. I could finally meet Josh. That sort of thing."

"So as far as you were concerned, you were only here in Canada to put on the show, nothing more?"

"That's right. However, at a certain point, I realised that Rupert was handling much more money than we needed just to put on the show. I knew of Rupert's connections, and some of them I didn't like. I started having my suspicions." He put the tip of a finger to his nose. "I can tell a *winkelhaak* from a windmill."

"Ah," Carmel said, uncertainly. "When did you first hear talk about radar sites?"

"On the day after the show, Rupert took me to one side and informed me of the plan to take a Russian agent up to Saglek. He kept saying how we could make a lot of money out of it, and so forth. I listened to all that he had to say and then said 'no dice'. He was furious. After that, we left each other, and at the first opportunity, I contacted the RCMP."

"Was that your first contact with them?"

"Absolutely. And I hope that when all of this is over, I'll never see them again. Or they me," he added as an afterthought.

"When did Valery arrive?"

"I would guess at about the time of the show, perhaps a little earlier. I never actually met him. Rupert and Gloria put him in a separate apartment. Gloria used to go over there in the grey Toyota to take him food."

"And Todd?"

"He appeared about then, maybe a little later."

"What role did he play?"

"He planned it all, and is now running the show. I still haven't met him in person, not even now, when they think I'm Rolf. We speak on the phone, that's all."

"When did Rolf arrive?"

"I suspect that Rupert brought him to Montreal at the very beginning. He must have been concerned that I wouldn't go along with their plan. In that event, they could get rid of me, and have Rolf fool Richard into thinking he was me. Once they were up at Saglek, Rolf could fool Josh as well."

Carmel paused, and an intriguing thought occurred

to her. When Gloria called Richard and got him to go to the condo just before the murder, was that in the expectation that Richard would believe the dead man to be Carlos? That way, he would then mislead the police into thinking the same thing? Was the trip that morning with Rolf in the car pretending to be Carlos simply intended to make it more likely that Richard would be fooled in that way?

She turned towards Carlos. "Tell me more about Rolf."

"I don't know much about him, really. He used to get work as a croupier at one of the casinos in Nassau."

"Ah! Maybe he was in the show. Richard told us there was someone running around with a cardboard roulette wheel over his head. Could that have been him?"

"I just don't know. Gloria organised all of that."

"Tell me what happened on the day of the murder."

Carlos took a deep breath and looked at her. "You're certainly giving me a grilling, aren't you? It's your job, I guess. I must say, you're pretty good at it."

Carmel smiled briefly. "Thanks."

"Yes, the murder. Let's see. That afternoon, the three of us met in the condo to divide the money from the show. After that, I had understood that we were going to fly to Toronto, and then take a second flight to Nassau. Rupert was very rude to Gloria and insisted that she couldn't have any share of the take. He wanted most of it for himself. He said that after all, it was thanks to him that we had received all that money from Todd."

"Rupert seems to like money."

"Rupert? He doesn't hive with drones."

"So, on the afternoon of the murder..." Carmel reminded him.

"Yes. We had our little argument about money. Gloria then left. She had several boxes of food that she wanted to take over to the other apartment. Rupert may have gone with her, I don't really know. He certainly helped her take the boxes down to the garage where she kept the car. After that, she was supposed to come back to get me."

"The elevator wasn't stopping on the ground floor that day," Carmel observed. "When I arrived later on, after Richard called for the police to come, I had to go up by the stairs."

Carlos looked genuinely surprised. "So it was Richard who contacted you. You may have said that before. How come? What was he doing there? How did he know that something was going to happen?"

"Gloria called him. She told him to go quickly to the condo, for your sake. She thought that you were in danger. So he went, and it was he who came across the body, and thought it was you. He then called us." Carlos looked at her, but said nothing. "Gloria didn't call you to warn you?" she asked.

He looked at Carmel with surprise. "Well no! If she had called me, I would have cleared out." He seemed puzzled. "No. Gloria didn't call me. And she never told me that she had called Richard."

"Do you think that Gloria brought Rolf in the car, or would he have come by himself?"

"I can't say for sure, but it seems to me more than likely that she brought him in the car. After all, she was waiting with the car when I went down, and that can't have been more that ten minutes after the shots were fired."

"So she wanted you murdered?"

Carlos looked up sharply. "No. I refuse to believe that."

"Where were you at the moment of the murder?"

"I can tell you exactly. I was sitting alone on a sofa in the living room with the door shut. Suddenly, I heard gunshots out in the hall. Three, I believe. Bang. And then a little later. Bang. Bang."

"Like that? With a pause between the first shot and the other two?"

He rubbed his chin thoughtfully. "Yes. I would say so."

"How long? One second. Three seconds? Five?"

"More like ten."

"Very loud?"

"Not really."

"Were you surprised?"

"Of course I was. I had no reason to expect anything of the sort. I was simply waiting for Gloria to come get me and take me to the airport." He said these words with such frankness that Carmel was close to being convinced. Then, she remembered that Carlos was a professional actor, and decided to reserve judgement. "What did you do when you heard the shots?"

"At first, I didn't move. I watched the door and listened for a key turning in the lock. I was afraid someone would appear. It's just possible that I heard some noises outside in the hallway; I can't say, really."

"And then?"

"After two or three minutes, I got up, picked up my briefcase, opened the door a crack and peered out into the hall. There was nobody there. Apart, of course, from the body."

"Did you realise who the dead man was? Did you know it was Rolf?"

"Not at all. I barely looked at him. I just wanted to get out of there fast."

"Was the elevator waiting for you when you left the apartment, or did it have to return from another floor?"

He thought for a moment. "I remember having to

wait for it. It seemed to take for ever."

"So you went down in the elevator. To which floor?"

"To the garage. Gloria was standing there."

"Was she surprised to see you?" Carmel asked.

Carlos hesitated. "I don't really know."

"Did she say anything to you?"

He paused. "Yes. In fact, she did. She said 'Carlos. Thank God you're safe!' She gave me a quick kiss and put me into the car, the little grey one."

"Carlos. When Richard arrived a few minutes later, he found the door to the apartment open. You have just said that you shut it." Carmel looked at him expectantly.

He tilted his head to one side and tried to remember. "I know! Gloria went back up to get something in the condo; a laptop, I think. She must have left the door open after leaving. I waited for her in the car. I was pretty much in a state of shock."

"And then?"

"I didn't really know what Gloria's position was. With the others, I mean. I asked her what had happened, and she said very little, just that the dead man was Rolf Sloman, and that he had come in order to kill me. We quickly left the garage, and then she stopped the car in a quiet street some distance away so that we could have a talk. I asked her why Rolf wanted to kill me, and she explained the whole thing to me, the plot to get someone on to a radar site up north and to use Rolf to pretend he was me. You can imagine how I felt about that."

"Yes I can."

"We discussed turning the tables on them by pretending I was Rolf. She felt that they would get out of the country fast when they learned that it was Rolf who was killed. I saw an opportunity to get even with Rupert, whom I detest, and she agreed to go along with the idea. I think her patience with Rupert had reached the breaking point. She left me off somewhere in the east end of Montreal. I stayed around for a few days avoiding the others and then came on up to Labrador."

"Whose idea was it first? This idea that you should pretend you were Rolf?"

"It just seemed to come naturally. To both of us, I mean. At the same time."

"After that, you continued to speak to the RCMP?"

"Yes. And at the same time, I kept in telephone contact with the others, so that they would go ahead with their plan. Pretending I was Rolf, of course."

"You say that the four of them are already here in Nain?"

"Yes. Where, I don't know. But it's a small place, so you should be very careful."

"Will you join them?"

"Yes, as long as I can just deal with Todd. Rupert would recognise me, of course." Carlos raised a hand and rubbed his forehead. He was getting tired. "Where are Richard and Emma?" he asked. "I hope they're not up here with you. For God's sake, don't take them up to Saglek. It's going to be far too dangerous."

"I haven't said I'm going to go to Saglek," Carmel said. "But don't forget there's Josh. Who's going to look out for him?"

"Yes. I hadn't forgotten Josh. I'll ask the RCMP to do their best to protect him."

"How many Mounties will there be, do you know?"

"They haven't told me, but lots, I hope. My God, it's cold in here!" He stood up. "Carmel. I've told you all that I can, and it's getting late. I wouldn't want the others to find you here with me. What do you think?" He took a tentative step towards the door.

Carmel decided to leave him in peace and rose as well. "I like your socks," she said. "Nice and cheerful. Did someone knit them for you?"

Carlos looked slightly embarrassed. "Yes," he finally replied. "Gloria did."

24

Carmel stood in the cockpit of Walrus, a flashlight in one hand and a marine chart in the other.

"Two points off east," Emma murmured beside her, adjusting their course and pushing the throttle forward to give Walrus more power. A tuque was jammed over her head, and her face, tinged with blue from the lights on the boat's instrument panel, looked tense and anxious. Beyond her, all was black, the velvety blackness of deepest night.

"Not so fast," Richard pleaded softly from the bow. He was sweeping a searchlight back and forth across the water to show the way down the passage leading out to sea from Nain.

Carmel glanced at the sky, her eyes travelling up the length of the Big Dipper until she found the North Star. It was almost directly over her head. She was on her way to Saglek—if the Mounties wouldn't take her, Walrus could!

The salt air was fresh on her face. She felt good, even if she hadn't had much sleep the previous night. The three of them had made a tight fit lying there side by side on the bunk in the bow of the cabin. Richard had wanted to ask her a lot of questions about Carlos, and what role he might presently be playing. They had planned to leave at daybreak, but already, at three in the morning, Emma was turning in her sleeping bag, looking out the window, taking the weather report, checking her watch. Finally, she had jumped up saying, "Time to go."

"Who'll be there, do you think?" Emma's voice sounded worried over the throb of the engine.

"At Saglek?" Carmel asked. "Todd. Rupert. Valery. Gloria. Plus the Mounties and, I would guess, Carlos."

"Those bums," Emma muttered. "Treating Richard like that. Trying to burn my house down."

"I'm glad we got Richard back in one piece."

"So am I. Now we have to do the same for Josh."

Walrus was beginning to rock slightly. They had passed between two small islands and were reaching open water, with its gentle swell. Carmel liked the feeling of the boat under her. It gave her a sense of independence. That, and the immense sky above. She was falling under Labrador's spell.

Emma's voice broke the silence. "Good thing you were there. I guess you learned to fight like that in the army."

"Yes," Carmel replied, absent-mindedly. "In the army."

"Maybe I should have done that."

Carmel turned to Emma. "Done what?"

"Gone into the army. You were in Afghanistan, weren't you?"

"Yes, I was. But why do you say you should have gone into the army?"

Emma peered at the chart and corrected their course slightly. "To be able to fight like that. To defend myself."

Richard called once more from the bow. "More to the

south, Emma. There's another island ahead."

Emma altered course once more. "Did you ever have to shoot at people, to kill people?" she asked Carmel.

"We were at war with the Taliban. We got shot at, and we shot back. That's normal."

"Do you think you killed anyone?"

Carmel became impatient. "Look. I was in the army. We were assigned missions. Patrol this village. Clear out that valley. We did all we could to achieve our objective, and to stay safe. Yes. We killed people."

"Anyways. You can sure handle yourself. That kick to the knee. He'll never forget it. What's his name?"

"Todd."

"He got what he deserved, trying to burn my house down. An eye for an eye and a tooth for a tooth. That's what I think." Emma pushed more on the throttle and Walrus surged forward.

"Some of us got killed in Afghanistan, too," Carmel said softly.

"I can imagine. People you knew?"

"My boyfriend. We were going to get married when we got out."

Emma turned to Carmel and laid a hand on her forearm. "Oh. I'm very sorry."

"No. It's okay."

The swell had become more pronounced, and Carmel could feel drops of salt spray hitting her face as the boat rose on the crest of a wave and then fell with a smack into the trough beyond. The lights of Nain twinkled far astern, looking like the fireflies she used to chase on hot summer evenings at the farm when she was a child.

She thought bitterly of the moment when they had brought Jean-Claude's remains back to the base. She had been washing her hair, trying to rid it of all that sand and dust. After that, she hated Afghanistan, and couldn't wait to get home.

They bore on through the night, silent now except the occasional call from Richard at the bow. Carmel's thoughts turned to Carlos, lonely and cold in his room at the hotel, waiting for events to unfold. His description of the three shots, one followed shortly afterwards by two others, agreed with what Sonny had told her—that one shot seemed to have come from a certain distance, and the two others from closer by.

The implication was that at the time of the first shot, the murderer had been farther from the victim, which meant that he was almost certainly hidden behind the plasterboard partition, and not standing in the doorway of the condo or emerging from the elevator. This, in turn, seemed to exonerate both Carlos and Gloria. Why would Carlos have waited in hiding behind the partition when he wasn't expecting trouble? And how could Gloria have possibly reached the place of hiding behind the partition before Rolf arrived by elevator, when they had only just arrived together in the garage below?

A rosy glow had appeared in the east, spreading up through the pale light above. "Red skies at morning, sailors' warning," Richard said to them as he returned from the bow. Emma reached her arms out to him and he gave her a long kiss.

Daylight came, and they had a breakfast of sandwiches and coffee in the cockpit. "What was Canada doing in Afghanistan, anyway?" Emma asked.

"It was a political decision," Richard said. "Canada wanted to show support for the Americans, after 9/11."

"But finally, did we achieve anything?" Emma asked.

"Not much," Carmel said. "We should just have clobbered Al-Qaeda and got out. Instead, we got bogged down, trying to sort out all their problems.”

“Where were you? In Kabul?” Richard wanted to know.

“Kandahar, mostly. Canada’s job was to hold Kandahar Province, pacify it, exclude the Taliban fighters.”

“That can’t have been easy,” Emma observed. “Did you get into regular battles with them?”

“Not usually. It was endless patrols and skirmishes. No set battles.” Carmel gestured with her hand. “Not like at Waterloo.”

“Waterloo?” Emma asked.

“The battle,” Richard said. “Where Napoleon was defeated.”

“The movie you saw in Montreal,” Carmel added.

Emma was clearly puzzled. “The movie I saw in Montreal?”

Carmel looked quickly at her. “Yes. Napoleon. You told us that you went to see it at the Forum Cineplex.”

Emma sounded irritated. “Oh. I remember now. On Thursday afternoon. It wasn’t very good.”

Richard offered to take the helm so that Emma could go below to catch some rest. “Thanks, Richard,” Emma said to him softly, tugging him to her before disappearing below.

Carmel watched her go, deep in thought. Emma had clearly told Sonny and her that at the time of the murder, she was watching a movie on Napoleon at the Cineplex Forum. Now, she had almost forgotten having done so.

This set her thinking about her own position. All along, Carmel had accepted Emma’s alibi. She had also accepted her hospitality. They had rescued Richard together; they were making their way north to Saglek together. You could say that they had become quite close. Had Carmel failed to keep a proper distance from Emma so as to retain her objectivity? There was nothing that connected Emma to the murder. And yet. And yet...

There were several unresolved questions in Carmel's mind. Emma had said she was single and had no family, and yet she had given birth by C-section. She had quit teaching after only a few years, for reasons never fully explained. Carmel had found her evasive when she asked her about the photo of her and a friend, standing under some palm trees, that hung in the house in Makkovik. Was it possible that the friend was Gloria? They did look a bit alike.

The sun had appeared from behind the clouds, and Carmel went to stretch out on a seat of the cockpit and have a nap.

Walrus advanced slowly northwards. The tree line was behind them now, and they had come to a land where all was rock and tundra. The coastline was increasingly mountainous and barren, with sheer cliffs and jumbled rockslides that fell directly to the water's edge. There were narrow fjords that snaked their way inland, disappearing into dark valleys, and the occasional iceberg floated by, heading south on the Labrador current. All along the way, they were obliged to edge past underwater rocks that barely appeared above the surface, flashing white where the waves broke over them. "Pinnacles," Emma called them.

Emma eventually reappeared from below and replaced Richard. She checked their position and examined the shoreline with her binoculars. "That must be Okak," she said. Richard went forward to sit on his favourite spot at the bow, and Carmel stood beside Emma at the console.

"There's an iceberg way ahead, a huge one," Richard shouted back to them. They altered course so as to pass close by. The iceberg was about sixty metres long and towered above them. It was coloured in shades of white and turquoise, and bore strange vertical flutes. A deep blue horizontal line traversed its base from one end to the other. "Magnificent," Carmel murmured.

"Yes," observed Emma, taking a quick look as she steered past, "but in a few weeks, it will have melted and be gone. Nothing lasts for ever, I guess."

Carmel looked at Emma. Her face was pale and she looked tired. "Do you think we'll make it all the way to Saglek today? It still seems quite a distance on the chart."

"No. We'll have to stop somewhere for the night." Emma jabbed her finger at a spot on the chart. "Maybe here, at Hebron. If we're lucky. Then tomorrow, it will be a short run up to Saglek Fjord. We can leave good and early."

"Anyway, we're doing pretty well," Carmel said. "You're a good skipper!"

"Thanks," Emma said to her briefly.

Carmel had a thought. "The other day, Emma, I couldn't help noticing that you once had a C-section. What happened?"

Emma frowned. "I didn't think it still showed." Her face tightened, and she seemed annoyed. "Yes, if you must know. That was when I was a lot younger. In the end, I lost the child. It was premature."

"That's very sad. I'm sorry. Was it then that you quit teaching?"

Emma just shrugged, and Carmel left it at that. She could see that she had touched a raw nerve.

The light began to fail, and the three of them kept their eyes on the coastline, wondering where they could find a decent spot to anchor for the night. At the mouth of Hebron Fjord, they explored westward, and found a sheltered bay where they could see a small number of abandoned houses scattered up a verdant slope. Emma had a look through her binoculars. "That's Hebron," she said. "It was the most important Inuit village up here in the old days."

"What's that big white building?" Richard asked.

"That must be the mission building. It was built by the Moravians almost two hundred years ago. They seem to be restoring it, doing repairs."

They approached the shore, and Richard went forward to drop the anchor. "What's the depth?" he asked Emma. "I can't tell how deep it is." Emma looked at her instrument panel and said that it was four metres.

Carmel found it hard to believe; the water was so perfectly clear, even in that light. On the ocean floor she could see hundreds of creatures—starfish, sea anemones, shellfish... There were also numerous rockfish, ugly sand-coloured fish with large heads and spiny backs that darted about near the bottom, or simply lay camouflaged on the sand.

Emma was busy looking at something else. She was staring anxiously at the shore nearby, and seemed upset, very upset. "We're going to have to take turns keeping watch tonight." Carmel and Richard looked, and at first saw nothing. It was hard to judge distances in a landscape without trees, and it was some time before they saw them on a barren island not three hundred metres away. Polar bears, two of them, climbing about on the rocks beside what looked like the rotting carcass of a dead whale.

WALRUS

25

Carmel stopped to let the others catch up. The mountainside was rough and steep, and now that they had reached their destination, all three agreed that they had no time to spare.

Richard and Emma were some distance below. He was standing on a large rock, catching his breath, his profile framed by the silver waters of Saglek Fjord. Emma stood just above him, knee deep in a carpet of stunted blueberry bushes and Labrador tea. She was shouting at him to hurry up. Below them in a shallow cove, Walrus swung back and forth on its anchor chain. The small red canoe which served as its tender lay bottom up on a big flat rock comfortably above the water's edge.

The skies were grey, and a chill wind blew in from the east. Out to sea, a bank of clouds lay low on the horizon. Or was it fog? Carmel wasn't sure. She zipped up her jacket.

Above her towered a massive cliff, its face cracked and weather worn. Off to her right, a cascade of rocks and boulders stretched from the base of the cliff down to the water's edge.

The other two reached a spot just below Carmel, and she pointed out a deep notch between two high cliffs that lay above them to the left. "I think that's where we go," she shouted. "In between those two cliffs. From there, we should be able to see the runway, and also the radar site."

"Let's go," Emma cried, and once more, the three of them headed up the mountainside. After scrambling over a series of short rock faces, they found their way into the entrance of the notch. Its floor was strewn with piles of shattered rock fallen from above, and the going was slow and difficult. "This is a land for giants, not for men," Carmel thought. However, the way gradually opened in front of them, and brought them to a long shelf of bare rock perched high above a broad rocky valley. The view from there was spectacular.

"There's the runway," Emma exclaimed. It lay at their feet, perhaps a half-kilometre away. It was a short runway and stretched off to their right on slowly rising ground.

"And look, there's the radar," Richard said, pointing to a dull white globe, partially shrouded by cloud, that sat on the summit of a mountain about one kilometre beyond the runway. "No planes anywhere," he added. Shielding his eyes, he scanned the skies to their south.

Carmel borrowed Emma's glasses, and took it all in, first the landing strip, and then the three buildings that lay on its further side. There was a parking apron at the near end of the runway. Beyond the apron was the rusty ruin of a dilapidated industrial shed, some sixty metres long, its windows smashed, and three openings appearing where once there must have been large sliding doors. At each end of the shed stood a separate, smaller building, still in a decent state of repair, and apparently, still in use.

Emma took back her binoculars and swept them back and forth. "I can't see anyone," she said, "but there's a four wheeler parked outside the right hand building. That must be the staff house, where Josh stays. The other small building at the other end must be the guest house, for visiting military."

Richard continued to scan the horizon to their right. "Listen!" he shouted. "Isn't that the sound of a plane?" The three looked anxiously to their south. "Sounds like a Twin Otter," Emma agreed. They started off again down the hillside, as fast as they could go.

The plane came in fast and low at the southern end of the runway, its landing lights blinking. They could hear a scream of rubber as it touched down, and then the roar of its engines as the pilot put the propellers into reverse thrust. The plane came to a near stop, and then slowly taxied down the runway towards the parking apron.

A man emerged from the door of the staff house and walked out to meet it. "That's Josh," Emma shouted. She started yelling at him, and waving frantically, but he was too far away to notice. The three kept on down the slope, with Carmel in the lead.

Carmel was less that a hundred metres away when the passengers of the Twin Otter disembarked. She counted four persons, and thought she could recognise them as Todd, Rupert, Valery and Gloria. There was no sign of Carlos. Josh walked casually out towards them, and although Emma kept shouting her warnings, the noise of the plane's engines drowned out her voice. As Carmel watched, Rupert went up to Josh and grabbed him suddenly by an arm. Josh tried to break free, but Rupert was too strong for him.

Todd arrived a moment later, limping badly, and took Josh by the other arm. Gloria and Valery then joined them, and there seemed to follow some sort of a discussion. Gloria had shoved all her hair up under a yellow tuque, and Valery was wearing a red jacket that looked several sizes too big for him. Rupert started pointing at Josh's four wheeler.

Carmel was less than thirty metres away from them when Todd noticed her. He shouted something and seized Rupert by the arm, pointing in her direction. Carmel dodged behind the Twin Otter. She didn't have a specific plan. It was going to be up to them to make the first move.

The air suddenly began to vibrate with the throb of a helicopter's rotors. The H145 arrived in a tremendous rush, and when it was immediately overhead the Twin Otter, it climbed sharply in a tight circle, and tilted hard on one side. The noise was deafening. Carmel could see a face in one of the windows. She hoped it was Jim.

Rupert and Todd were clearly rattled, and Josh managed to wriggle free. He ran towards Carmel. "Follow me," she shouted to him with a wave of the hand, and together, they rushed over to the right-hand opening of the long industrial shed, the opening that was closest to the staff house. Once in the shed, she had a quick look at him. He was slight but wiry, his face was broad and flat, and his hair was jet black. He had a moustache, a little one, not bushy like Sonny's.

"I'm with the police," Carmel shouted to him. "Stay here, and you'll be safe." The shed was cluttered with bits of old metal, and Carmel chose herself a length of pipe that was lying on the ground, weighed it in her hand, and rushed back with it to the doorway of the shed.

Emma and Richard arrived, and Emma threw her arms around Josh and tried to explain what was going on. "She's police," she shouted over the noise of the helicopter, pointing at Carmel. "The Mounties are coming in to land. They want to arrest the others, the ones who tried to grab you at the beginning. Stay with us."

"And stay in here," Carmel shouted to them from the doorway of the shed.

She looked down the side of the long shed and saw Valery and Todd running towards the opening at its far end. When they reached the opening, Todd looked desperately about, shouted something, presumably to Rupert, and then disappeared with Valery into the shed. Further away, Rupert and Gloria were arguing. He had her by the arm, but she broke away and ran off towards the door of the guest house. He chased after her.

The helicopter came down in the middle of the apron with a thud and a bounce, and two RCMP officers jumped to the ground. One of them was Jim. Carmel ran out to the edge of the apron. "Another 'copter coming?" she shouted, over the noise of the rotors. He shook his head and made a gesture of hopelessness with his arms. "Delayed," he shouted back. "Got here too late." She couldn't believe it. In Montreal, for an operation like this, they would be a dozen.

"There's two of them in the end building," she yelled, pointing over towards the guest house. "Two others went in there." She indicated the far opening of the shed, forty metres away from where they were standing.

"Can you help?" Jim asked breathlessly, ducking out from under the rotors and joining her at the edge of the apron. "Got a gun?" He didn't wait for an answer, but thrust a Smith & Wesson into her hands. "It's loaded. And here are some handcuffs. I'm an optimist."

He pointed to where Todd and Valery had gone. "Let's get those guys first. You go up through the shed, and be really careful." He pointed to the second Mountie. "I'll stay outside with Matt."

Jim and Matt pulled out their weapons and headed cautiously along the outside of the shed, while Carmel ran back inside. "Stay put," she told Emma, Richard and Josh. She turned to look down the interior of the shed.

"What a junk yard!" she said to herself as she picked her way around army trucks and snowmobiles, bulldozers and steamrollers, all of them rusty relics of the nineteen-fifties and nineteen-sixties. Having a revolver in her hand felt good. It was reassuring, even if she hoped she wouldn't have to use it.

She tiptoed past the second large doorway, and the junk got even harder to get through. There were rock crushers and excavators, jack hammers and generators. Then came a collection of old jeeps, with US Army markings, all crammed together, and the remains of a blue dump truck. She was going more carefully now—the third opening, the one where Todd and Valery had gone, was getting closer.

Edging past a rusty tangle of used metal reinforcing bars, she bent low and peered ahead under the wreckage of a discarded jeep. Close to the ground, there was something bright red. It had to be Valery! She shifted to one side to have a better look. Now she could see his red jacket. He was huddled under an oil tank.

Carmel looked carefully around, but there was no sign of Todd. She went slowly towards the end of the jeep, and seeing that Valery was unarmed, stuffed the pistol back in her pocket. She would need both hands to catch him.

Valery was now three metres away. He glared at her from his position under the oil tank and started screaming insults at her in what sounded like Russian. A moment later, he popped out from under the oil tank like a rabbit from its burrow. He tried to get by her, but she stuck out a leg and grabbed the back of the red jacket as he went by, swinging him up off his feet and over on to the hood of the jeep. "Gotcha!" she shouted, smacking him down good and hard. He tried to twist away, but he was winded and there wasn't much fight in him. In a moment, she had his two wrists handcuffed behind his back.

"Got one of them, Jim," she yelled. "With the red jacket. Watch out for the guy who limps."

She dragged her prisoner out of the shed and back to where Richard and the others were waiting in a state of great excitement. Emma was holding Josh by the arm, wanting to stop him from going outside to join the fight. Richard was standing by the opening, brandishing a heavy metal bar.

Carlos was there as well. He must have come in on the RCMP helicopter.

"Sound the tucket. Ho!" he shouted to Carmel in apparent encouragement. He was clearly enjoying the action.

Carmel thrust Valery into Richard's arms. "Hang on to him," she panted. "Don't let him go." She charged off to rejoin Jim.

Jim and Matt were waiting outside the third opening of the shed. "We can hear him," Jim yelled, pointing inside. "He's in there somewhere. Cover us, Matt." Matt dropped to one knee and held his pistol aimed at the opening of the shed, while Jim and Carmel cautiously spread out and approached it, Jim to the left and Carmel to the right. "Come out with your hands up," Jim shouted.

The next moment they heard a shot from their left, and Matt keeled over, grabbing his left arm with a curse. Jim swung left and fired several shots, and Carmel saw Rupert, pistol in hand, disappearing back through the door of the guest house.

Carmel ran up towards the opening of the shed, firing a warning shot in the air and shouting, "Come out with your hands raised." An instant later, Todd rushed out holding a gun on her. After a couple of steps, his knee gave out on him and he fell to the ground, firing a shot harmlessly into the air. A moment later, Jim landed on top of him and wrenched the pistol from his hand. "Thanks," Carmel shouted, as the two of them put handcuffs on Todd, who was kicking furiously, and swearing at them in some foreign language.

Matt had picked himself up and made his way over to the helicopter, where the two pilots were putting what looked like a tourniquet on his upper arm. Jim went over to speak to them, while Carmel dragged Todd back to where Richard was keeping Valery. Richard quickly passed Valery over to Carlos and took charge of Todd.

Carlos was in high spirits, and stood over Valery, hefting a nasty-looking length of iron rebar. Carmel overheard him explaining to Richard that he planned to sell out in Nassau and return to Montreal. She took an anxious glance in Emma's direction. She was at the back of the shed, talking nervously with Josh. Carmel rushed back to speak to Jim.

"Matt's bad," he said to her, "and we've got the two we're really after. Also, the weather's socking in. I'd like to send Matt and the two prisoners down to Goose Bay right away in the Twin Otter."

Carmel agreed and went to fetch Todd and Valery. Todd was fuming with anger and barely able to walk, whilst Valery seemed bewildered and apathetic. Jim explained what he wanted to the pilot of the Twin Otter, and within a moment, the plane had Matt, Todd and Valery on board, and was taxiing off down the runway, heading for Goose Bay.

Jim and Carmel now went cautiously back towards the guest house, staying close to the shed in case they needed to take cover. When they arrived, they separated and went to either side of the entrance. "You in there," Jim shouted. "Come out with your hands up." A moment later, Rupert appeared at the door, holding Gloria in front of him as a human shield. She appeared to have taken a nasty blow on the forehead, and was bleeding badly. Her yellow tuque was soaked with blood.

Seeing the two armed police officers approaching from either side, Rupert shoved Gloria ahead of him and darted back into the building. Gloria stumbled and fell to the ground.

Carmel kept her pistol trained on the building, watching to see where Rupert might have gone. A moment later, a shadow appeared in one of the windows. She rapidly put three shots through the glass, and Jim did the same with a volley of his own. The sound of the fusillade echoed round and round in the surrounding mountains. Jim continued to cover the window as Carmel ran up to Gloria and helped her back onto her feet.

"Give me your gun," Carmel said, reaching into Gloria's pocket and pulling out a small pistol. "Now let's go, fast." She took Gloria by the arm, and they ran back to the helicopter, where all of the others were now gathered.

The sight of Gloria, stumbling along beside Carmel with her face half covered in blood, was too much for Emma. "Glo!" she screamed, rushing forward in a storm of tears. "Emma," Gloria cried. The two fell sobbing into each other's arms, while Carmel stood panting nearby, looking on with a sinking feeling in her heart.

26

Jim came up to Carmel and laid a hand on her shoulder. "Thank God you were here," he said. "Without you, Matt and I would be dead by now." He was trying to look calm, but his hand was trembling. "Thanks, Carmel," he said. "Thanks, a ton. Really!"

She was still catching her breath. "We were lucky they split like that, two of them in the long shed and the other two in the house. That made it a lot easier."

Jim nodded. "We have to leave now," he said. "The woman with the injured face needs to see a doctor. I'll take Carlos as well." His hand tightened on her shoulder. It felt strong, and their eyes met. "What about you?" Jim asked. There was an expression of impotence on his face, and Carmel knew why. His orders were not to take her back with him.

She gave him a weary smile. "Thanks, Jim. I have to stay. I'll go back with Emma on her boat. You can ask the other two what they want."

She took a step back and reaching into her pocket, pulled out the Smith & Wesson, and handed it to him with a short smile. "Thanks for the loan." She patted her other pocket. "Here's another one. I took it from Gloria, the woman who is wounded. Make sure you put it in a safe place somewhere. It could be important."

Jim took the pistol from her and looked at it. It was quite small, and the grip was powder blue. "A Walther," he said.

"So it is. May I see it again?" She took it back, removed the ammunition clip, and had a close look. "Same kind of bullets as were used in the murder. You'd better send it down to my boss in Montreal, Sonny Samuels. Tell him it could be the weapon that was used to murder Rolf Sloman."

Jim returned to the helicopter with the pistols and then went to speak to the others. Carlos and Gloria were already sitting in the back of the helicopter, and Richard and Josh both chose to stay with Emma and return by boat. Jim came back to have a last word with Carmel. "Are you sure?" he asked. "Will you be alright?"

"Yes, we'll be fine. Thanks, Jim."

"I'm only going as far as Nain. Josh says he has an emergency transponder. If anything goes wrong, just turn it on. I'll keep an eye out for you. And stay away from that other guy."

"Rupert?"

"Yes. Rupert. We can pick him up later. He's not important. Please leave him to us."

Jim returned to the helicopter, and after giving her a last, anxious look, climbed on board. A moment later, the rotors started to turn and Carmel found herself standing there with Emma, Richard and Josh as the helicopter lifted off the ground, tilted, and headed south under a lowering sky. She had never felt so far from anywhere in her entire life.

The air was turning colder, and she reached into her packsack to bring out another layer. She could feel the effects of the recent firefight in her back and shoulders. More than anything else, however, she was haunted by the image of Gloria and Emma as they hugged each other. To her, that embrace had tragic implications. She missed Sonny and wished he was there for her to talk to.

Emma was looking pale and tense. "They got out just in time," she said. "The weather's changing."

Richard bent over to pick up his packsack. "We'd better get back to Walrus right away." The four of them shouldered their packs in silence and headed out across the runway towards the mountainside. Josh knew of the spot where they had left Walrus, and so they let him lead the way.

When they reached the crest of the mountainside, it started to snow. Not heavily, but just enough to remind them where they were. Josh led them through the notch, and then down the further side towards the bay where Walrus was anchored. Fortunately for them, the snow stopped, and for a while, the sun even appeared under the clouds to their southwest. They found the little canoe, and Emma paddled Carmel and Josh out to the boat, and then returned to get Richard.

Out to sea, a heavy fog bank had cut across the eastern horizon like a curtain of cotton wool. It was gradually coming closer to shore. Emma was worried. "No way we can leave for Nain with fog like that, and we're far too exposed to the weather in this little bay. We're going to have to find a proper place to anchor, and fast." She and Josh looked at the chart and agreed on a long inlet further to the west, on the north side of the Fjord. Emma took the wheel and soon, they had left the south shore behind them. Carmel stood at the console beside her.

Emma was looking straight ahead, and her face had taken on a remote, far away look. Her hair was swept back under her tuque, making her profile, the long straight nose and the square chin, all the more striking.

"You should have gone back with the 'copter," she said to Carmel.

"I couldn't. Jim had instructions not to take me."

"Oh." Emma remained silent for a while.

"At least Jim's happy," Carmel said. "He has his arrests. An arms dealer. A Russian spy. Enough to keep the Mounties busy for quite a while." She tried to sound cheerful about it all, but her heart wasn't in it. She had her own job to do now, and the prospect gave her no pleasure at all.

"What will happen to Gloria?" Emma asked.

Carmel glanced at her. "Why? Are you worried about her?"

"Well, no. Why would I be?"

"She has become a material witness in the murder of Rolf Sloman." Carmel looked intently at Emma's face to see if the name would provoke a reaction.

Emma took a while to respond. "Is that the name of the man who was murdered in Montreal?" she finally asked. "Instead of Richard's brother?"

"Yes, it is. His name was Rolf Sloman. He apparently was a friend of Rupert and worked as an entertainer on the cruise ships."

Emma's face remained without expression, but her voice dropped to a hush. "I see," she said.

"I think that the others, Todd and Rupert, brought him to Montreal. Rolf Sloman was also an actor and happened to bear a certain resemblance to Carlos. The plan was to have him pass himself off as Carlos, and persuade Richard, and later on Josh, to help them get onto the radar site."

Richard had now joined them and was listening intently. "If it was Carlos who killed him, that would be in self-defence."

"Yes," Carmel answered, "but I don't think it was Carlos." Richard started to ask why, and she interrupted him. "I have my reasons for saying that."

"You think she did it," Emma stated, her voice flat and emotionless.

"Gloria? I'm not saying that at all. But when we arrested her just now, I took a handgun from her. I have sent it down to Montreal to have it tested."

"Tested for what?" Richard and Emma both asked the question at the same time.

"To see if it was the same gun as the one that killed Rolf Sloman. I expect that it was. Same caliber. Same ammunition. If so, Gloria will have a lot of questions to answer."

There was a long silence, and Carmel turned and left Emma alone with her thoughts. Josh quickly took her place beside Emma. He knew Saglek Fjord well and wanted to point out the way ahead.

Richard was up at the bow, and Carmel went forward to join him. "You must be tired," he said to her with admiration. "They were damn lucky you were there to help."

She nodded. "It was close. Too close."

"You should have gone back with them. Why didn't you?"

Carmel sighed. "Richard. Prepare yourself. I stayed because of Emma."

"Because of Emma?"

"Yes."

"You think she may have had something to do with the murder, is that it?" he asked anxiously.

"Yes. That's it." The two remained silent for a while. "Richard. There's something I need to know," she said to him in a low voice.

He caught the seriousness of her tone. "Certainly. If I can help."

"Thinking back to the show Carlos put on in Montreal, would either you or Emma have seen Rupert or Gloria that evening?"

"I certainly didn't, and I don't think Emma did either. She was with me all the time."

"Did either of you recognise any of the actors out on the floor?"

"Again, I certainly didn't." He thought for a moment. "At one point, Emma stood up. She seemed surprised by something. I think it must have been one of the actors."

"She stood up?"

"Yes. We were seated, and then she suddenly rose to her feet and stared down at what was happening on the floor of the arena."

"Did she say anything?"

"No."

"What was she staring at? Do you remember?"

He hesitated. "It must have been the man with a cardboard box over his head."

"You mean the box shaped like a roulette wheel?"

"Yes. A roulette wheel."

Carmel nodded in silence. That would have been Rolf, she now felt sure.

Carlos had said that Rolf had worked at a casino in Nassau. Somehow, Emma had recognised him. That meant that she had known him previously. Something dramatic must have happened between them at some point in time. If she could find that out, she would learn who had murdered Rolf Sloman and why.

In less than twenty minutes, they had reached the inlet which they had chosen as an anchorage. The water was not very deep, so they were obliged to anchor some distance out from shore. They had themselves a quick supper on board. They were all exhausted, and no one said very much. After that, they went ashore.

The beach was a long strand of rock and pebble, marked by patches of dark sand and piles of leathery green seaweed. Here and there were small rock pools, left behind by the ebbing tide.

Josh produced a small tent from his packsack, and Richard helped him set it up by a stream that flowed into the bay at one end of the beach. Richard agreed to sleep on Walrus, and Emma, Josh and Carmel set themselves up to spend the night in the tent. There was still a bit of light, and Carmel and Emma went for a walk along the beach together. Carmel could tell that Emma was on edge, waiting for Carmel to ask her the inevitable question.

"Emma," Carmel began. "I couldn't help seeing that you and Gloria are close."

Emma said nothing.

"You should be the one to tell me. Please, for your own sake. I'll find out one way or the other. So you tell me. How long have you known each other?"

Emma looked straight ahead. "Eight or ten years, I suppose."

"How did you meet?"

"Like that. Common friends."

"Where?"

"In Nassau." Emma's voice broke. She was nearly in tears.

Carmel continued. "Did you also meet Rupert at that time? Were he and Gloria already married?"

"Yes. It was about then that they were married."

"Did you also meet Carlos?"

"Not that I can remember."

"What about Rolf Sloman?"

Emma stopped and turned to Carmel. They stood there facing each other in the receding light. Emma placed both hands on Carmel's shoulders and looked at her. "Give me time, Carmel," she pleaded. "You keep asking me all these questions. I don't know what to say, and what not to say. Please, Carmel. Give me time."

27

That night, the fog came in and wrapped itself silently around their tent. Several times, Carmel had an anxious look outside. It certainly didn't look like they were going to be able to leave on Walrus the next day.

Daylight confirmed her fears. The fog was still present, and grey skies pressed down on them, flattening the landscape and shortening the horizon. On the water's surface, wraiths of fog came and went, tantalising them by seeming to dissipate, only to return twice as thick as they had been before. Emma came over to stand beside Carmel, shaking her head. "Not today," she said.

Carmel heard Josh calling to them from the hillside above and turned to look. He was running down towards them, pointing his finger at something out on the Fjord, beyond the inlet where Walrus was anchored.

It was a small speck that gradually grew as it approached amongst the patches of fog. Emma took a look with her binoculars and then passed them to Josh. "What is it?" she asked him. He took a look.

"It's that old canoe that was kept down on the beach

beyond the airstrip," he said after a while. "Someone must have left it there. That's weird. There's someone in it; a man, I think."

Emma looked at Carmel, her face working with alarm. "What if it's Rupert?"

Carmel took the binoculars from Josh and looked out over the water. "It could be him," she said slowly. A cold feeling started to spread down her back.

"We have to warn Richard," Emma exclaimed, and ran down towards the beach, shouting "Richard!" repeatedly. Carmel and Josh followed her, shouting as well. However, there was no sign out there on the water that Richard could hear them. He had their red canoe with him; they could see it, laid flat on the roof of the boat's cabin. He himself they could not see. He was inside the boat. Perhaps he was still asleep.

The man in the canoe approached Walrus slowly, as if he didn't want to be observed. Emma had a long look at him with her binoculars. "That's Rupert alright," she said. They watched with alarm as he reached Walrus, carefully tied his canoe to a stanchion, and went on board. He disappeared into the cabin, and for a minute or two, they were left in the dark as to what was happening. Finally, he emerged, pushing Richard ahead of him. He appeared to be holding a gun to Richard's back. Emma gasped, her face in her hands.

Richard took a seat in the bow of the canoe, and Rupert unsteadily climbed into the stern, still holding his pistol. The two took up paddles and made a slow progress towards the beach. Carmel's hand instinctively moved to her hip, but she was unarmed. The only thing she could think of was to play for time and avoid a confrontation.

"We have to try to speak to him," she said to Emma and Josh. "It's our best chance. Speak to him, and above all, not get him excited."

When the canoe reached shore, Rupert left it at the water's edge and, giving Richard a shove in the back, indicated that he should join the others. He himself stopped at a certain distance from them, pistol in hand. Richard walked over to where Emma stood and wrapped an arm about her shoulders, his face dark with anger. The four of them stood there together, facing Rupert.

"What do you want?" Carmel asked Rupert after a moment.

"Whose boat is that?" Rupert replied, speaking aggressively, and gesturing over his shoulder towards Walrus.

"Mine," Emma replied uneasily.

"Yours?" Rupert turned towards her. "That's your boat?" He gave her a second look. "I know you. You're Emma! What the fuck are you doing here?"

Emma looked at him. "I live here. In that house you tried to burn down, you bastard." Rupert seemed taken aback. "And what about you, Rupert?" she asked. "What are you doing here?"

He gave no answer, and Emma continued, her voice gradually swelling. "You have no business here, you and the others. You shouldn't be here at all. And I'll tell you what, Rupert. The others have been arrested and taken down to Goose Bay. They're the lucky ones. You, you're finished! You'll never get out of here alive." Her voice rose to a shout and her eyes flashed as she pointed a finger at him. "You should never have come, and you'll never go back."

Carmel held Emma by the arm, hoping to stop her from provoking Rupert and making matters worse. "What do you want?" she asked Rupert once more.

He turned towards her. "Who are you?" He took a

second look at her. "Aren't you the woman who crashed into our car on the road to Goose Bay? Was it you who threw that bottle back at me? What's it all about? Who are you, anyway?"

"I'm Carmel Roch," she said. "I'm with the Montreal police. If you surrender to me now, I can guarantee you that you'll be dealt with fairly."

"Montreal police, my ass. Keep your hands away from your pockets, or I'll put a bullet through you. Right away." He looked at them all menacingly. "Who called the cops on us, then? How come they showed up like that, just as we got out of the plane? Which one of you did that?"

"Carlos did," Emma said.

"Carlos?" Rupert glared at her. "Carlos? You're crazy. He's dead." All the same, a hint of uncertainty crossed his face.

"No, Rupert," Emma answered, with a bitter laugh. "Rolf is dead, not Carlos. That was Carlos at the landing strip with the Mounties. Couldn't you tell the difference?" She taunted him. "Maybe you were too busy to notice, hiding in the end building and beating up on Gloria."

Rupert gave her a furious look, and she spoke once more, in a lower voice, with intensity. "You're good-for-nothing, Rupert. You're a failure. You've always been too stupid to know what's right for you." She was getting really angry now, and the words came boiling out. "You loved Gloria, and yet you couldn't stop beating her, so that now, she has finally turned against you. You had a good thing going with Carlos, the club, the theatre, all of that. And yet you robbed him, and planned to kill him, and now, he has brought the Mounties down on your head."

He stood there, silenced by her outburst. Carmel tightened her grip on Emma's arm. She didn't like the situation they were in at all. It was far too explosive and unpredictable.

"Carlos did that?" Rupert finally asked. "He called the cops on us?"

Emma laughed bitterly. "Yes, and you were too dumb to catch on. You thought it was Rolf leading you on up here, but it was Carlos. And where are you now, Rupert? You're on the run in northern Canada, without a friend in the world. Rupert! You've completely fucked up your life. Do you realise that?"

Rupert glared at her. "I haven't given up yet," he shouted. "That's your boat? Then you're coming with me. You and I are going to take a little boat ride back to Nain."

"Not without the others."

"No. They stay here. You can send a plane for them."

She shook her head. "I won't leave without them."

"Yes, you will." He pointed his pistol straight at Emma. Carmel squeezed her arm. "Don't move," she whispered.

Josh had shifted imperceptibly towards their left. Rupert gave him a quick, worried look. Richard had also edged slightly away from them, on the other side. He now left Carmel and Emma, taking a short step towards Rupert, his arms spread out wide. "Come on, Rupert," he said. "Be reasonable. Let's talk."

There was a moment of frozen silence as Rupert stared at Richard and then took a step back. Slowly, he raised his right hand and a shot rang out, shattering the stillness. Richard collapsed onto the beach, clutching his chest. Rupert spun around and sprinted back towards the canoe with Carmel and Josh in close pursuit. Splashing frantically out into the shallows, he pushed the canoe ahead, leapt in, and paddled furiously towards Walrus.

Emma screamed, "Oh no!", and threw herself onto Richard's body. She took his head in her hands. "Richard," she pleaded. "Say something." He closed his eyes hard, as if to shut out the pain in his chest. Emma looked hysterically up at Carmel, who had run back to join her. "What can we do?" she asked several times. She started kissing Richard furiously on the lips. "I love you, Richard. I love you!"

Richard's eyes opened, and he looked up at Emma and gave her a faint smile. "I'll be alright, Emma. Don't worry." He tried to continue talking, but his voice trailed off and the smile faded. He had a spasm of pain, then another and another. His face was pale, and his body started to go limp. A trickle of blood appeared in the corner of his mouth. Emma burst into tears and hugged him, entreated him, but it was no use.

Carmel kneeled down beside Emma and held her close. They remained together like that, Carmel holding Emma and Emma holding Richard. "You will be cold here, Emma," Carmel said to her after a long while. "Come back to the tent. Josh will bring Richard."

Emma shook her head and held Richard's body to her own. She was making low noises, keening, her body rocking back and forth. "Richard," she whispered. "My baby. Stay alive. Please. It's my fault. It's all my fault. Richard. My baby. I'm sorry. I'm so sorry." She was in tears, unconsolable, and started beating the ground with her fists.

28

Josh carried the body up to the tent, and prepared a bit of flat ground nearby where he laid it on its back, the arms lying neatly by its sides. The wound was barely visible. Josh had stanched the blood with a piece of cloth and placed a handful of fresh Labrador tea leaves on top. He then started to place rocks around the body, flat rocks, some of them sizeable. Emma moved closer to Carmel. "What is he doing?" she asked her in a whisper.

Josh explained. "In the old days, we buried our dead this way. There was no way to dig into the ground, so this is what we did." He continued to add more rocks, selecting the best ones to place around the head and feet. Gradually, a low wall of rocks rose before them, with Richard's body lying within.

Josh stood back, his hands on his hips, looking at the makeshift grave. Richard was to be buried in the manner of the Inuit. Carmel saw that the body was facing south. She wondered if Josh had done that on purpose, and if so, whether south represented Montreal or Makkovik.

When he had completed the ring of rocks around

the body, Josh fetched several large flat stones to place on top. He rolled them like cartwheels over to where they were sitting, and when he had collected several of them, he turned to Emma and took her by the hand. He wanted her to have a last moment with Richard before he completed the grave.

Emma understood and went over to the body. She kissed Richard's hands and face several times, and knelt there beside the body for a long while, the tears pouring down her face. Then she rose to her feet. On an impulse, she removed her wind jacket and laid it on top of Richard's body. "To keep you warm," she whispered.

Carmel and Josh stood close behind her. Josh had a fresh branch of Labrador tea in his hand and placed it on Richard's body. Carmel reached down and picked up some pebbles, which she placed beside the branch. Emma then looked over at Josh, her eyes blurred with tears, and nodded her head.

Josh selected each large flat stone in turn and leveraged it up and over to form the top of the grave. Carmel found the stones enormous and marvelled at his strength. After the burial, each of them stood silently apart, and Emma finally took refuge in the tent.

Carmel looked occasionally out across the water to where Walrus was riding at anchor in the bay. Sometimes, she saw Rupert moving about in the cockpit. Their red canoe was still lying on the roof of the cabin, and the other one was tied up to the boat and turning back and forth in the water beside it. That was reassuring. The water was far too cold for Rupert to swim to shore. As long as the two canoes were in sight, Rupert had to be on the boat and could pose no immediate danger for the three of them.

She guessed that Rupert would be considering what

his next move should be. She doubted whether he would be able to run the boat by himself. Emma had the ignition key with her. In addition, it would be very difficult for someone who was not familiar with Walrus to open the feed lines, turn on the electronics, start the engine. No, she decided, Rupert would not be able to operate Walrus without Emma's help.

Josh left them after a while and walked further up the hillside beside the stream. When he returned, he spoke to Carmel. "There is a better place for the tent up there." He pointed well up the slope. "We should move." Carmel understood at once. If they were to spend the night in peace, they should be far from the beach. Rupert would not dare to come looking for them in the dark if there was any risk of one of them getting behind him and making off with the canoe.

They took down the tent, and Josh led them up the hillside to their new location, which was hidden from Rupert's view by a fold in the bedrock. Once the tent was set up, Emma crawled back into her sleeping bag.

Meanwhile, Carmel and Josh opened the four packsacks to check their food reserves. There was not much—some bread, a tin of sardines, several apples. Josh said nothing, but reached into his bag and pulled out a short stick with some fishing line wrapped around it. There was a lure with a treble hook embedded into one end of the stick. He laid it carefully to one side. "To catch fish," he explained to Carmel.

Carmel remembered Jim telling her that Josh was also carrying a transponder. She asked Josh to get it out. He emptied his bag in front of them, and from the bottom, out fell a cylindrical object, fairly large and obviously quite heavy. It was an old-fashioned personal locator beacon. Once activated, it would send out a distress signal giving their location. Hopefully, the signal would be picked up by Jim down in Nain.

Josh looked at Carmel. "Should I turn it on?" he asked. She nodded for him to go ahead. He looked about and chose a large rock nearby, setting the transponder on top of the rock and turning on the switch. A little light came on, and he turned to Carmel with a satisfied look on his face and gave her a thumbs-up.

After a short while, Josh picked up the stick with the bit of fishing line wrapped around it and headed up the hillside. Carmel took a quick look into the tent. Emma was fast asleep, so she followed Josh up the hill to see what luck he would have.

He waited for her to catch up with him and led her to a little pond that was a part of the stream system that went past their tent and down to the beach. Picking up a stone the size of his fist, he told her to watch closely. He then threw it into the pond. A black swarm seemed to cloud its surface and move swiftly away from where the stone had fallen. "Fish," Josh said.

He explained that the char were on their way up to a lake to spawn, but were waiting for more rain or snow so that the stream would fill. He then unwrapped the fishing line from the stick and threw the lure into the pond, pulling it back sharply once it had sunk to the bottom. On the third try, he snagged a fish by the belly and hauled it rapidly onto the bank. It was easily big enough to feed the three of them, twice over.

That evening, Josh gathered some twigs and branches and made a small fire by the tent. Carmel fetched Emma, and the three sat in silence, eating the fish. After that, Carmel and Josh went out to explore their surroundings and pick a few berries. Down towards the beach, they came across several spots where the short grass had been trampled. Carmel pointed them out to Josh. "What happened here?" she asked.

"*Nanuk*," he replied, looking about and whistling softly to himself. "Three or four. They slept here."

"What?" Carmel was alarmed. "What are you saying?"

He pointed at the grass. "Nanuk. Polar bears."

"When? When were they here?"

"Two nights, maybe three nights ago."

A feeling of nausea rose in Carmel's stomach. Bears! Like the ones they had seen at Hebron. What should they do if one appeared? Run or stand fast? Run where? "Shouldn't we put our tent further up the hillside?" she asked Josh.

He shrugged. "We just stay quiet, and if they come, we stay together and make a lot of noise." He looked up at the sky, testing the wind. "I don't think they know we're here. They could be far away by now."

"Please, Josh. Don't tell Emma what we saw," Carmel said to him, as they returned to the tent. "She's bad enough as it is."

Some time in the middle of the night, Josh looked outside. "Come see," he said to Carmel and Emma, opening the door of the tent. "*Arsaniit*. The northern lights."

Carmel got out of her sleeping bag and went outside. Endless patterns of colour were flickering across the blue-black sky. They were mostly white and green, and constantly shifted back and forth, from directly over their heads to all the way down to the horizon. The sight seemed to suggest dancing, or music. "The spirits of the dead," Josh said softly to Emma, who had joined them.

Emma fell to her knees. "Richard," she sobbed, and broke into tears.

Carmel felt overcome by it all, the solitude of the place, the dangers that they still faced. She reached a hand down and placed it on Emma's shoulder. "Emma," she said. "Try to think that Josh is right. Try to believe that those are the spirits of the dead, welcoming Richard into their midst. Think of it that way."

29

Morning dawned grey and heavily overcast. The hills behind their tent were dusted with a light sprinkling of fresh, wet snow, imparting a raw dampness to the air. Out in the bay, Walrus rocked at anchor, occasionally swinging to one side or the other as the wind shifted. There was no sign of Rupert, but the two canoes were visible. They picked a few berries to eat, and then sat on some rocks by the tent, finishing the last of their bread. Emma seemed somewhat rested, and she and Carmel exchanged a few words. "Richard was a very decent person," Carmel said.

"Yes, he was wonderful," Emma answered quietly. "Not like so many of the others."

"I liked what Josh said about the spirits of the dead. It seems to be such a happy explanation."

Emma smiled softly. "Happy for those who die. It's harder for those who don't." The two lapsed into silence.

It was about nine o'clock in the morning when Josh stood up and, shading his eyes with one hand, stared out over the water towards a small island beyond where Walrus was anchored. "Let me have your glasses," he asked of Emma. They were all looking now.

"What do you see?" Emma asked him, rising to her feet.

He handed her back the glasses. "*Nanuk*. Polar bears." Carmel's heart froze. She stared out across the water.

"Where?" Emma asked, raising the binoculars. After a moment, she drew in a sharp breath. "I see them. Up on that little island." Josh nodded.

Carmel took the binoculars and found the island. High up on the rocks, she saw a yellow-white blur. It appeared very small, but that was because it was so far away. A kilometre or more, she guessed. The blur was moving slowly across the rocks. Then she saw something else that was moving. "I think I see a second one," she said. "What do we do, Josh?"

He didn't answer at once, but kept looking out across the water. "There's three of them," he said. "Two are on the island, and a third one is in the water, swimming out from the shore."

"Which way are they moving?" Emma asked anxiously. "Shouldn't we go up the hill?"

Carmel glanced back at the long mountainside that lay behind. "That might be better," she said. "We could go up there."

Josh didn't answer right away. Once more, he was following the bears with the binoculars. "Don't move," he cautioned. "They can run faster than we can. They are young bears," he added. "Those are the most dangerous. They know no fear." The suspense grew. "The one who is higher up on the rocks is standing now. He's big!"

Josh passed the glasses to Emma. "What do you think?" She took a quick look, then passed the glasses back to him with a shrug. "Wait," he said. "We should wait here, and stay quiet."

They lay on their stomachs on a long flat stone partially masked by some blueberry bushes and remained perfectly still. Josh continued to describe the scene for them. "The ones who were on the island have left it and have returned to the shore. They seem to be coming in our direction. The one who was swimming has joined them. They've stopped now." He fiddled with the focus of the glasses and looked once more.

"The closest one is on his hind legs again. He has his nose up in the air." Josh sounded excited. "He must have smelled something."

Emma raised her head to have a better look. "Smelled what?" she asked.

"Something on Walrus," he answered.

The three watched in fascination as the bears ambled slowly along the shore towards a point opposite where Walrus was anchored some fifty metres out into the water. The bears were now clearly visible to the naked eye and looked ponderous and threatening. The first one splashed out into the water, heading towards Walrus. The other two followed slowly behind. Carmel looked sideways at Emma, who was white as a sheet. "Can they climb onto the boat?" Emma asked Josh anxiously.

"Easily," he replied.

The first bear reached Walrus and they could see its huge head, dripping wet, as it rose up alongside the boat. "It's biting the hull," Carmel said to herself. "It's actually biting it." She could see a piece of wood ripping away from the gunwales.

The second bear now arrived to join the first, and placed a paw on the boat, which started to sway and swing about. Carmel stole a look at Emma. She was sucking her lower lip. "There's Rupert!" she suddenly exclaimed.

Rupert had emerged from the cabin, wearing what

looked like a blue track suit. They could see him start back with surprise, and then look desperately about for something with which to defend himself. His hair was a black tangle, and he scrambled about in the cockpit, waving his arms. Carmel could see his mouth opening and shutting, but from where she was, his shouts were inaudible. She stole a quick look at him with the binoculars and almost regretted it. He was gibbering. She had never seen a face so distorted by fear and horror.

Two of the bears had now placed their front quarters on the near gunnel, and Walrus was listing badly and taking on water. Rupert tried to stand on the roof of the cabin, but the red canoe was in his way. He picked it up and threw it at the first bear. It literally demolished the canoe with a stroke of its paw. "Jesus," Emma muttered.

The other canoe was in the water, attached to the boat on its further side. The third bear arrived on that side and tried to climb up on it. Carmel saw the canoe fold in two and disappear beneath its weight. The ends resurfaced further on and floated away, two crumpled tangles of wood and fibre glass.

The third bear dove under the boat and joined the other two, adding its weight on the gunnel. Walrus rocked sluggishly and sank deeper into the water. Rupert took up a paddle from the floor of the cockpit and brought it down hard on one bear's paw. The paddle broke, and he was left holding its shattered end. "What will he do?" Carmel wondered. "Will he jump into the water?" Of course he wouldn't; it was far too cold. In any event, it wouldn't do him any good.

The first bear now thrust itself out of the water at the stern of the boat, its wet fur lying flat along its flanks and a flood of water pouring off its back. It leveraged itself up over the transom, and the boat's bow rose violently in the

WALRUS

air. The bear lunged into the cockpit, collected itself, and rose on its hind legs to confront Rupert, who had retreated onto the roof of the cabin. For a moment, Rupert looked over to the hillside where the three of them were watching, as if he meant to plead for help. The bear lowered its head, bared its teeth, and sprung at him.

A high, piercing scream travelled across the water as the bear bit through Rupert's leg just below the knee. To the naked eye, he seemed for the briefest of moments to be doing a dance, but then he fell and disappeared from sight. The three bears crowded over him, the fur of their heads and shoulders staining pink with blood. Carmel looked away. She couldn't take it any longer.

Josh moved slightly beside her, his eyes fixed on the bears. He was making a soft, chanting noise in low, guttural tones, tapping two fingers on the rock to mark the rhythm.

On her other side, Emma didn't move. She stared out over the bay, her features hard and implacable.

30

The wind got up that night, shifting to the west and bringing colder temperatures down from the north. None of them slept well. Carmel had listened as Emma moved quietly beside her, and noticed each time that Josh went outside to have a watchful look around. She herself lay there most of the night unable to sleep, a vein in her inner ear pounding maddeningly, her mind full of the events of the last several days. She was very worried by what lay immediately ahead.

Everything now depended on their being rescued by the RCMP. Walrus existed no longer; the bears had seen to that. Once they had finished with Rupert, they had torn the boat apart, searching for food. First, it was the instrument panel. Then they got into the engine compartment. To Emma's horror, the roof of the cabin was slowly detached from the rest, and finally, the contents of the cabin, bedding, kitchen utensils, books, assorted bits of fabric and of plastic, all were flung overboard in a frenzy of ruin and destruction. When the marauders finally swam away, Walrus was nothing but a submerged hull, barely visible in the dark waters around.

It was Josh who spoke first as they lay there side by side in the tent, waiting for the morning to dawn. "The weather is changing," he said. "Today it will clear."

"Is your beacon still transmitting?" Carmel asked.

"Yes," he said. "I checked."

"Will it be clear enough for a helicopter to fly?"

"Yes. If it's like this down in Nain as well." Josh got up and went out of the tent. He wanted to catch more fish.

Carmel turned in her sleeping bag and looked worriedly at Emma beside her. She smiled and asked Emma how she felt.

Emma gave her a wan smile. "I'll be OK." She raised herself on an elbow. "Carmel. I've been thinking about what to say to you, and how to say it."

Carmel nodded. "I understand."

"It has been complicated. Now, in a sense, it has become more simple."

"What is it that you want to tell me?" Carmel asked her gently.

"Carmel," Emma finally spoke. "I want to say something first. Something that can help explain the rest. I told you that my father was in the army. What I didn't say was that he was discharged from the army, for drunkenness and violence." She said nothing for a while after that, and Carmel herself remained silent, waiting for what might follow.

"I was twelve when he left the army. We were living in northern Ontario. My mom did what she could, but it got worse. He would go away for a few days at a time, and then return and stamp around the house, beating things up, beating my mom up too, and sometimes me."

"She should have reported him, I can see that now, but she didn't. It was as if she thought that my father's behaviour was simply normal."

Emma sounded angry now. "Yes! She should have reported him. She should have turned him in. But she never said a word to anyone. Even when it was my turn to get hit, she pretended she hadn't noticed. How can a mother not notice when her daughter is crying her eyes out behind her bedroom door, and comes out later with a ripped T-shirt and a black eye? How can a mother not be on her daughter's side? Why do women always think that men are right, that they can do what they want?" She clenched a fist and pounded it on the floor of the tent.

"Mom and I moved back to Saint John's, where she continued working as a nurse while I studied and finally got my teacher's certificate. My father died in North Bay. His liver did him in."

"Carmel. I'm telling you this just so you'll understand." Emma started to pull herself out of her sleeping bag. "I need to go outside."

They both dressed, and Carmel followed Emma out of the tent. It was daybreak, and to their north, they could see the summit of Mount Caubvick gleaming white in the morning sun.

Emma disappeared behind a rock for a moment, and then the two of them walked slowly down the hillside to Richard's grave. They paused there for a while, and then set out along the beach. "The other day, you asked me if I knew Rolf Sloman."

"When my mother retired, we took a cruise together in the Caribbean. On the boat, I met the man who was in charge of entertainment, and we started to see a lot of each other. He was amusing, he danced really well, I was on a cruise. I fell in love with him." Emma turned to Carmel with a bitter smile. "Mom didn't think much of him, and told me I was a fool. She was right."

"Rolf?" Carmel asked.

"Yes. Rolf. We said goodbye in Miami at the end of the holiday, and Mom and I went back to Saint John's. Not long afterwards, I discovered I was pregnant."

"Mom was in favour of an abortion, but I was excited by the idea of having a baby, and decided to keep it. The more it grew in my belly, the more I wanted to keep it. I made up names for it, started collecting clothes, that sort of thing. I asked around and found out that Rolf had left the cruise ship and taken a job in Nassau. I flew down to see him. By then, I was over four months pregnant."

"I found Rolf and moved in with him, but it was a disaster. I loved him; he didn't love me. I wanted the child; he didn't want to have anything to do with it. We made love, but it wasn't like before. He got rough with me. Time passed."

As they walked on, Emma became increasingly agitated. She didn't look at Carmel. She punctuated what she was saying with a hand in the air, and sometimes with a clenched fist.

"Those were desperate days for me. I met Gloria, though, and we became friends. She was going with Rupert. He and Rolf used to see a lot of each other. I was there when Rupert and Gloria got married. My belly was pretty big at the time, but I wasn't the one who was getting married."

"Shortly after that, Rolf and I had a big fight. He hit me, and he hit me again. I did everything to protect my belly, to protect my baby. By then, I knew I was expecting a girl. That really excited me. He left the apartment, and as I later learned, he left Nassau. He even emptied my purse as he went, the bastard. I felt I was going to go into labour, even if I was only in my sixth month. Gloria came and stayed with me. She was wonderful."

"At the hospital, they did everything they could. I had to have a C-section. The baby came, and I called her Rosemary. Like the herb. They kept her in the special ward for premature babies. After four weeks, Rosemary died. She was normal, just terribly premature. She didn't have to die. She could have been here with me today."

Emma's voice broke. A moment later, she was sobbing desperately. She took Carmel by the shoulder and pulled her close, and for a while, they clung to each other on the beach. "I'm sorry," she said after a while, wiping her eyes.

"Don't worry," Carmel said, wanting to calm her. They walked on together, avoiding the waves as they came running up the strand to flow about their boots.

"The rest, Carmel, you know. Or can guess at. I quit teaching. I hit a low. Mom died, and that didn't help. I knocked about a bit, became a fishing guide. And met Richard."

Emma stopped and turned to Carmel. "The last thing I expected when Richard took me to that show was to see Rolf. But there he was, out there on the floor."

"With the roulette wheel over his head." Carmel added.

"Yes. And half naked. I was pretty sure it was him, even if he had put on some weight since we had last seen each other. The next morning, I returned to the arena and found Gloria, who was in charge of cleaning up. We were really happy to see each other again. She said yes, it was Rolf."

"Glo and I saw each other several times over the week, and she told me everything. I decided to speak at least once to Rolf. At first, I just wanted to tell him what a bastard he had been, nothing more. Gradually, however, my old rage came back to me, and when I learned that on Thursday afternoon, he was going to kill Carlos, I decided to go myself and stop him from doing so. Gloria was terrified that it would somehow go wrong, that Rolf would try to kill me too."

"So she lent you her pistol?"

"That's right." Emma took a deep breath.

"I went to the building where Gloria said it was to happen, hid behind a partition outside the apartment where Carlos was staying, and waited. I must have been there for an hour or more before Rolf came up in the elevator. He was alone. I stepped partly out from where I was hiding and called out his name. He turned to look, and recognised me. He swore at me, said foul things, sort of laughed at me. 'This is it,' I said to myself. 'It's now or never!' I pulled out the pistol and fired a shot at him. I think it caught him in the back, because he had started to turn away from me. He fell flat on his face, but he was still moving."

"And the two other shots?" Carmel asked.

"I went up to him, where he was lying, and fired one shot into him for Rosemary, and another one for my mother. Then I took the elevator down to the garage, where I saw Gloria. That was a surprise; I wasn't expecting to see her there. I guess she must have brought Rolf there in her car. There was some kind of a bag in the elevator. She took it and threw it into a bin that was standing nearby. I gave her back the pistol and left the garage as quickly as I could, on foot."

"What were your feelings? And how do you feel about it now?"

"I was perfectly calm afterwards and felt happy with what I had done. I still do. I have no regrets, no more than I feel sorry for what happened to Rupert yesterday."

They returned to the tent and ate some fish, and then moved all of their belongings down to a flat area near

Richard's grave where they spent several hours clearing rocks, making the area as level as possible, so that it would be a good place for a helicopter to land. Josh piled all the rocks that they removed onto Richard's grave in order to make it more bear-proof.

Josh heard it first. To start with, it was just a throbbing, a pattern of reverberation in the air, hardly a noise at all. Then it grew, and they could see a small speck that rapidly got bigger as it crossed Saglek Fjord coming towards them, hugging the water, not wishing to lose visual contact with what lay below. It reared up above their heads like a gigantic spaceship, the pilot tilting the helicopter this way and that, looking for the right angle to bring her safely down. They stood to one side and waited as the helicopter placed itself gently on the ground in front of them.

The door opened and a man's head appeared. It was Jim. "Are you alright?" he shouted anxiously over the noise of the rotors. He looked around. "Someone's missing. And the boat. Where's the boat?"

He ducked down under the rotors, which were still turning, and came out to join them. Carmel briefly explained what had happened. He nodded. "Let's get you on board. You can tell me all about it later. We stop to refuel in Nain and then continue on to Goose Bay."

Carmel and Emma slept most of the way south, and Josh left them in Nain. When they were approaching Goose Bay, Emma asked if they could stop by her house to collect a few things, and Carmel agreed. "And then?" Emma asked. "I suppose you'll want me to go down to Montreal with you."

Carmel smiled wearily at her. "Yes please, Emma."

31

Carmel felt emotionally and physically exhausted when she headed for work the next morning. Charles Gagné had met them the previous day at the airport in Goose Bay, and the three of them, Carmel, Emma and Charles, had been whisked off to Montreal in an unmarked jet, arriving at midnight. There, they were met by Perras, who left Carmel off at her door, and disappeared with Charles and Emma into the night.

All night long, she had relived those moments, those terrible moments, when Rupert had shot Richard, and when he had then met his own fate. Could she somehow have saved Richard's life? Hour after sleepless hour, she searched for an answer, but found none.

Walking to work helped her regain a certain peace of mind, but then she started to ask herself how she would draft a report on the murder, how she would relate the facts incriminating Emma as the murderer. Would she be able to do it at all, she wondered. "Emma," she almost cried out loud as she rounded the last corner before reaching the police station, "Emma, please forgive me!"

Two black limousines were pulled up outside the station, surrounded by a swarm of police cars with their red lights flashing. A group of men dressed in business suits and carrying briefcases emerged from the building and hurried past her into the limos. Carmel thought that one of them looked like the Minister of Justice, but she wasn't sure.

The girl at reception came out from behind her desk and gave Carmel a noisy hug. "Carmy! Thank God you're back!" In other circumstances, Carmel would have laughed. It was as though she was returning from another life, on another planet. "They're expecting you," the girl added. "Upstairs. In the conference room. The big one."

"Right now?" Carmel asked. "Who?" She wondered what was going on.

Carmel took the elevator up to the top floor. She couldn't remember when she had last been there. Not recently, in any event. The conference room was in the middle of the building and had no windows. There was a long table, lined with chairs on each side, and some large paintings on the walls.

Charles Gagné and Emma were there, sitting at the far end of the table. Emma was staring at her hands, pale and bleary-eyed. She had been crying. Charles looked awkward, embarrassed even. Carmel wanted to go up to Emma, to embrace her, perhaps say something by way of apology or consolation, but Emma didn't even look up. Carmel was cut off from her, she was shut out. She chose herself a chair halfway down the long table, feeling miserable and discouraged, and waited.

A noise came from the hall outside. Sonny appeared in the doorway with a woman at his side. She entered the room with an icy calm, chose a chair directly opposite Carmel, and sat down. It was Gloria.

She was wearing a charcoal grey pantsuit with wide lapels and a ruffle of cream-coloured silk at the neck. Her wonderful hair was braided and piled high on her head like a golden crown. She looked marvellous, even if there was a discreet bandage above her left eye.

"Once more, we meet!" she said to Carmel. "I'm so happy to see you again." There were no soft edges; everything was remote and businesslike.

Sonny turned back towards the door and hung a do-not-disturb sign outside before closing it. He came over to Carmel and hugged her briefly. "Thank God you're back, safe and sound," he said in a low voice. He then went to the head of the table, gave a little cough and took his seat. Carmel thought she had never seen him looking so tense and unhappy.

Carmel glanced down the table to Emma, but their eyes didn't meet. She then turned towards Sonny, who was in the process of opening a slim file that he had placed on the table in front of him.

"On Monday, September 28, 2023," she heard Sonny say—or rather read—"forces of the Goose Bay detachment of the RCMP followed a Twin Otter to Saglek, in the Province of Newfoundland and Labrador, and arrested Valery Shtiskin and Genadi Todaglù, as they were in the course of carrying out a plot to sabotage a radar site of the Early Warning System. A third person involved in the plot, Rupert Marsham, of Nassau, in the Bahamas, escaped arrest...." He droned on. Carmel stared at Gloria, who was nodding her approval to Sonny. For the rest, she remained supremely aloof, even Madonna-like. She had yet to look in Emma's direction.

"Her lifelong friend," Carmel said to herself with a jolt. "She hasn't even said hello to her." Emma was screwed down in her chair, her mouth partly open, mutely staring with a kind of fascination at Gloria.

Sonny continued reading. "Assistance in the arrest was provided spontaneously by Lieutenant Detective Carmel Roch of the Montreal Police, who was present at the site in the course of her investigation into the murder of Rolf Sloman, of Nassau, in the Bahamas, which murder occurred on Thursday, September 10, 2023, in the City of Montreal." This time, Sonny turned to Carmel, who sensed that she was being asked to agree, and mutely nodded her assent.

"Ms Roch had come to Saglek in a small boat, accompanied by Richard Seaton, of Montreal, and the owner of the boat, Ms Emma Sinclair, of Makkovik, in Labrador. Following the arrests, they, and the person in charge of maintenance at the radar site, Mr. Josh Atanak, also of Makkovik, took this boat to a place nearby, where they spent the night. The next day, the said Rupert Marsham appeared, and in the altercation which ensued, in the presence of all, he shot and killed Richard Seaton. On the following day, and once more in the presence of all, Rupert Marsham was himself attacked and killed by some polar bears."

Emma stirred at the end of the table. "Three bears," she murmured. Sonny paused to look at her and then made a correction to his document. He looked over at Carmel and gave her a fleeting smile.

"Rupert Marsham was a material witness in the investigation into the death of Rolf Sloman."

"So was Gloria, for shit's sake," Carmel was thinking. "Gloria, who put the gun into Emma's hand. Gloria, who waited for her downstairs after the murder." She looked across the table, but Gloria was staring at the ceiling, looking detached. "Who is she?" Carmel asked herself. "What is she doing here?"

"Without his evidence," Sonny continued, "it will be impossible to throw further light onto the circumstances of that murder."

There was a deathly silence in the room. Gloria was perfectly composed, and started to examine her finger nails. It was then that Carmel realised that her name had not even been mentioned in the report that Sonny was reading. Gloria was a non-person!

Her mind flashed back to the events of the past three weeks. Gloria, lending her pistol to Emma. Gloria, telling Emma about Rolf's plan to murder Carlos. Gloria, telling Richard to go to the condo, for Carlos' sake. Gloria, driving Rolf to the murder site. Gloria, meeting Emma in the garage afterwards and taking her pistol back. Gloria, hatching the idea with Carlos that he should pass himself off as Rolf. Gloria, accompanying the plotters to Saglek. Gloria, luring Rupert off to the guest house so that it would be easier for the police to arrest Todd and Valery in the long shed. Gloria, who was not even mentioned in Sonny's report.

Carmel looked over at Emma, who was in a daze, totally unable to follow the drift of events.

"For this reason, the investigation into the death of Rolf Sloman is closed." Carmel stared at Sonny as he shut the file in front of him with a snap. At first, she couldn't believe her ears. Then, she suddenly had a flash of intuition, of comprehension. For whatever reason, there was not going to be a trial. No-one was going to be tried for the murder of Rolf Sloman!

Gloria nodded her approval to Sonny. She glanced rapidly at Carmel and the others, stood up, and walked towards the door. Sonny rose as well and accompanied her out of the room.

Emma was by now crying uncontrollably, and Carmel

went over to her. Emma rose to her feet and closed her arms about Carmel. "What's going on, Carmel?" she asked through her tears. "What happened?"

Carmel whispered to her. She was so overcome by emotion, she could hardly find her voice. "You're free, Emma. There will be no trial. You're free to go home. You're free!"

She was shouting now, she was so happy. "You're free, Emma." She then remembered who and where she was, and stopped abruptly. Charles rose and led Emma out of the room.

Sonny had reappeared. He looked at Carmel uneasily. "I had to," he whispered. "They made me do it." He raised his arms to shrug and then dropped them back to his sides. "They didn't want the investigation to continue. They didn't want a trial. They didn't want her to have to testify. She's untouchable." There were tears of fury in his eyes.

Carmel's head was swirling as she headed down the stairs to her office on the second floor. Why was Gloria untouchable? Who was she? Her hand slid down the handrail as she descended, floor after floor. At the last landing, a shadow emerged from the obscurity and she heard her name being spoken. She stopped. It was Gloria. The only difference was that she had now hidden her hair under a cream-coloured beret.

"Who are you, exactly?" she asked her.

Gloria smiled. "Many things, Carmel. Just now, I guess I'm mostly Mrs Marsham, recently widowed."

It was then that Carmel knew. Suddenly, all of the pieces fell into place. Gloria had to be working for the Americans. She was probably CIA. She looked at her with a mixture of curiosity and respect. "I see," she said. "Yes. Now I see."

"I'm happy for Emma," Gloria continued. "Please

take care of her. Tell her that I'm sorry we can't see each other just now. Try to explain that I'm not all bad, that I'm not just a monster."

Carmel's face flushed with anger. "That won't be easy. She has lost Richard. She has also lost her boat. She almost went to jail for murder. She may not find it easy to rebuild her life."

"I know that." Gloria hesitated. "Things never work out quite like you expect. When you're dealing with people, there's always the unpredictable element. You have to exaggerate, to take chances. I guess that's one difference between what we do, you and I."

"Yes," Carmel said. "I have to maintain order, to protect people. With you, it's not so simple. The stakes are higher. There can be collateral damage."

"You're right, Carmel. Thank you for understanding." Gloria took a step forward and reached out her hand. "My car's below, waiting for me. I have to go." They shook hands. Then Carmel watched as Gloria went down the last flight of stairs and exited the building through a side door.

Carmel drew a deep breath. She had the giddy sensation of having nothing in front of her, no persons to interview, no reports to read, no lives to save. She headed for her office, wondering what she would do with the rest of her day.

I would like to thank Stewart Learning of Cartwright and Paradise River for the wonderful times we have enjoyed canoeing together in Central Labrador.

I would also like to thank Meg Graham for her helpful comments on an early draft of this book.

Finally, my thanks go to Paul Abraham for the cover and illustrations, and to The Aaxel Author Group for their editorial and technical support.